AMY WILSON

Snowglobe

Illustrated by Helen Crawford-White

MACMILLAN CHILDREN'S BOOKS

First published 2018 by Macmillan Children's Books
an imprint of Pan Macmillan
20 New Wharf Road, London N1 9RR
Associated companies throughout the world
www.panmacmillan.com

ISBN 978-1-5098-8580-0

3 5 7 9 8 6 4 2

A CIP catalogue record for this book is available from
the British Library.

Printed and bound by CPI Group (UK) Ltd, Croydon CR0 4YY

'I on't know what Amy Wilson has running
ugh her veins as she writes but I think it
t really be magic – Snowglobe is one of the
purely original and imaginative children's
s I have read this year. Literally spellbinding'
Pi s Torday, author of The Last Wild trilogy

'A parkling tale of love and friendship reminiscent
of Diana Wynne Jones's magical stories. Snowglobe
shii mers with warmth, family and fairytale magic.'
Pet r Bunzl, author of Cogheart

' the crowned queen of magical middle
. . I devoured it! Full of real emotion and
us imagery, with family and friendship firmly at
t' Sarah Driver, author of The Huntress trilogy

Vilson spins magic with her words. Spellbinding.
t. I loved it!' Eloise Williams, author of Gaslight

ost breathtakingly magical fantasy novel I've
a very long time' Stephanie Burgis, author of
ragon with the Chocolate Heart

Books by Amy Wilson

A Girl Called Owl

A Far Away Magic

Snowglobe

For my mum, Helen, and my children,
Theia, Aubrey and Sasha.

Prologue

There were three sisters, named for Jupiter's moons: Ganymede, Callisto and Io. As they had blood in their veins, so they had magic, fine and strong as a spider's web. They lived in a house of white marble, and the tower stretched to the sky and speared the clouds, searching, they said, for the moon. They filled it with miniature worlds, set whole galaxies spinning, caught within glass spheres. And then they hid in their house while the world changed.

That was their lot.

But lots can change, and change can be chaos.

Callisto was the first to go: she left for love and the laughter of a boy with hair as red as fire.

Io was next: she left for solitude, and found her home in a place none could ever change.

Ganymede was left alone in the house of infinity. She stalked the marble corridors, ruling over everything they had created with a hard eye.

The world never knew of these sisters. Their house went unseen, their stories unheard.

And then came chaos.

1

It's not like it's hurting. Not much. And the lesson is only ten minutes longer – I've been watching the clock – so he'll have to stop soon anyway. I try to ignore it, but it's *prod, prod*, at the base of my spine. *Prod, prod*, like a heartbeat, only not so regular.

It's science, and we're sitting on stools, so it doesn't take much for him to reach back from the bench behind and do it. One, two, *prod, prod*. I find myself counting the seconds between them. Ten, eleven, perhaps he's forgotten – *prod, prod*. Thirteen, fourteen, fifteen, *prod*.

I don't know why he took such a dislike to me. It was pretty instant, I remember, on the first day of school. He looked at me; I looked back at him. I tried a smile, but he turned and said something to his friend, and they both began to laugh. It took me a few seconds to realize the laughter was unkind, and the smile froze on my face, heat rushed to my cheeks and they laughed harder. They laughed at everything then. My clothes, my bag, my hair. He said my eyes were weird; that all of me was weird. I went in every morning trying not to be, hoping it'd be different. New bag, bright smile, same eyes – no difference. What was worse, he turned the laughter on to anyone who sat by me. Nobody sits by me now, except those who are made to in lessons.

It's OK. I read my books, smile at the new kids, hope, hope, it'll change.

It hasn't, so far. Doesn't matter how bright I make my smile; the weirdness shines brighter, I guess.

Mrs Elliott is talking about the homework, and I'm behind already, so I should focus. I try to listen, but *prod, prod* – it's all I can hear now, all I even am. It is *my* heartbeat, *prod, prod*, faltering and mean, *prod*. She's saying something about force, *prod*. And then there's a whisper, and a breath of laughter, and something breaks deep inside me, like a wishbone that's been pulled too tight and shattered into pieces.

'*STOP!*' I howl, whirling from my stool to face him just as he reaches out his arm again. I push it away

4

and something flashes, bright as lightning. His stool ricochets across the science lab, and he flies with it.

There's a terrible crashing racket as he and the stool land up at the far wall, and then a deafening silence. My ears are ringing; my head feels like it's been pressed in a vice.

'*Clementine Gravett!*' shouts Mrs Elliott. 'Mrs Duke's office, immediately!'

She charges over to Jago, who is in a little heap beside the now-broken stool. He stares at me, like he knows something. Like he's got something on me now. Like he knew all along I was a freak, and here's the evidence: he knows that wasn't ordinary; it wasn't just strength. The whole class is silent, and they watch without a word as I pick up my bag and head out of the room.

It was magic.

My mother's magic.

I've been pretending ever since my first day at secondary, ever since Jago first saw the weird in me, that it isn't real. The roar of my blood, the flashes of static – all just the fantasies of a daydreamer. When I was smaller, that was all it was. But ever since my eleventh birthday, it's been getting stronger, less dream-like.

And the last two minutes have changed everything.

*

'Tell me what happened.'

I can see from Mrs Duke's face that she really wants to know. I'm a quiet girl. I don't hit, or shout, or storm out of classrooms. I don't make a fuss. Sometimes my work is scruffy, sometimes my homework is late, and I don't have the best grades, but I'm not a troublemaker.

'I don't know.'

'Clementine, I can't help you if I don't know what's going on. This seems out of character . . .' She leans forward at the waist, looking at me intently. Her expression is so kind. I've never seen her like this before. Her office is pale with winter sun, and dust motes float around us. I hope I'm not swallowing them; I try to breathe through my nose.

'Clementine?'

I can't look her in the eye. I concentrate on the biscuit-coloured carpet and my black boots. They're scuffed, and the yellow laces are unravelling.

'Mrs Elliott was quite shocked,' she continues, resting back into the comfy chair again. We're in the informal bit of the office, away from her desk. The chairs are navy blue and scratchy. Her short silver hair shines in the sunlight coming through the window. 'She says you pushed him clear across the classroom. We were lucky he wasn't injured. *You* were lucky, Clementine.'

'I didn't mean to,' I say.

She sighs. 'But you did. And there are consequences.' She looks up at the clock. 'Your father is on his way. Perhaps we'd better not continue until he arrives.'

'He's coming?'

'We called him.' She nods, watching me closely. 'Is that OK?'

'Yes.'

I don't tell her I'm surprised he's coming; it might not sound right. I love my pa, but he's very absent-minded, and he tends not to do things other parents would do. Like come to school. He hasn't been here in so long I wonder if he'll find it. I wonder what he'll say.

'Mr Gravett, the stool *broke*,' she says some time later, her voice close to despair. 'Clementine is a good student,' her eyes flick over me again, as if to reassure herself that I really am. 'But we can't tolerate violence of any kind, and she has made no explanation.'

'Clem?'

His eyes are sorrowful as ever, his unbrushed hair standing up on end, like a burning match. He doesn't look like he belongs here. I guess neither do I. Maybe that's what Jago saw that first day, a year ago.

'I didn't mean to,' I say.

Mrs Duke sighs, tapping her fingers on the folder she has on her lap.

'I just wanted to stop him.'

'From doing what?'

They both lean in to me. And my mouth dries up. What am I going to say, he poked me in the back? It sounds ridiculous, like I'm five. I suppose I could talk about all the other things that have happened over the last year, but they're all so small, so silly.

He says I'm a freak.

He says it might be catching.

He shoves his chair out and tries to trip me, just as I'm passing with my lunch tray.

No.

I don't know how to explain it. I was different from the start, and it's lonely, even in the moments he's not there to taunt me. Surrounded by hundreds of people every day, and alone all the same. I overhear conversations, and in my head I join in sometimes, smile at a funny bit, and then I realize I'm just staring at people, smiling to myself. Or I have thoughts that want to be out there, and they just wedge in my head because there's nobody

8

to tell them to. Maybe I whisper to myself when I walk along the bustling corridors. Maybe I stare too much at other people. Maybe I drop books, miss balls, stumble on steps, maybe I just don't quite fit. Maybe that's why I bother him so much.

But I don't say any of that.

I don't say anything at all.

Mrs Duke raises her hands at my silence. 'I have no choice, Mr Gravett,' she says. 'Even if Clementine *had* some sort of justification, it wouldn't be enough. We have a zero-tolerance policy, and there is no question that she pushed Jago, hard enough to break his stool and throw him to the floor. She will have to be suspended.'

'Suspended?' Pa asks.

I blush. He probably doesn't even know what that means. He probably thinks they're going to hang me upside down on the nearest tree.

'She is not allowed on to the grounds of this school for two days,' she says, her voice crisp with frustration. 'We will expect her back next Wednesday, and not before. She may access the online portal to get her homework and any study notes.'

Pa blinks, and stares at her.

'I fail to see how that is going to resolve the issue between them.'

'We will have to pick that up on Clementine's return,' she says smoothly. 'I hope that over the intervening period, Clementine will have a chance to work out what *did* happen here today, and be able to articulate it so that we can work with her on a solution.'

Pa mutters something under his breath before springing to his feet. Mrs Duke flinches back into the chair – he doesn't look like he'd be so nimble.

'Come on, Clem,' he says. 'Let's go.'

He doesn't exactly smile at me, but there's a twinkle in his eye as he picks up my bag and swings it over his shoulder.

Mrs Duke stands and follows us out, frowning from the door as we leave – two little matches against a grey sky. We don't look like we fit because, sometimes, we don't. Pa may not have it in his blood, but he's known about magic for longer than I've been alive. And me?

I guess there's not much use in denying it now.

2

'This was your mother's,' Pa says, handing me a slim, leather-bound notebook. 'Perhaps I should have given it to you earlier, but I wanted to be sure the time was right.' He peers at me. He's a little short-sighted, but he never remembers to wear his glasses. Mostly they're parked in his hair.

'I'm sorry about today.'

'I know,' he says, pulling out a chair opposite mine and stealing a chip from my plate. 'It's not good to go throwing boys around classrooms. I'm sure there was a reason –' he holds up his hands as I begin to protest – 'but it won't be good enough, Clem. I've been trying to talk to you for a while now about your magic; you can't ignore it any more.'

'When did you try?'

'Last Sunday, I'm sure. And a few weeks before that as well,' he says absently. 'I know I'm not around enough, Clem. I'm sorry you don't have more. Perhaps the book will help in some way . . .' His voice trails off and the tormented look creeps back over his face. It's very difficult to be angry with Pa when he looks like he's already feeling about as bad as a person can bear to feel.

'It's fine,' I say. 'Thank you for the book.'

He looks from me to the book. 'It was never far from her.'

The notebook is made of leaf-green pitted leather, and it warms quickly in my hands. The cover is worn, the gold-rimmed pages within flutter softly when I look through it. My mother's handwriting is small and spidery. I trace my finger over the words, feel the way they were pressed into the page. She did that. My mother. It's about as close as I've got to her for more than ten years. She never let anyone take photos of her – she said it pinched her soul.

'I'll leave you to it,' Pa says, loitering by the door. 'But go careful. There's some big stuff in there.'

'Why did she go?'

I don't look at him when I ask it; I just keep my eyes on the book.

'Not because of you,' he says.

'So then what was it because of?'

'I don't know,' he says. 'I wish I did, Clem. One day perhaps we'll find out.'

She is the space between us, sometimes. We don't know how to talk about her.

The first page is a pencil sketch of a tall, thin house that stands alone in a valley. Shadows crowd in on every side, and it feels like there are dangers there, hiding in scribbled lines just out of sight – but the house itself is bright beneath a crescent moon. Balconies jut from first-floor windows, a tiny bridge curves between two towers high over the huge doorway and a dozen steps lead down into ornate gardens where flowers bloom pale against the darkness. It's a beautiful picture, and I can see the places where she lingered, the paper shiny with pencil strokes and scarred where the shadows are thickest.

On the next page, her name, *Callisto Paradis*, and then pages and pages of the close-set writing, scrambled together to make the most of the paper. There are rhymes and wards against curses between fragments of thought, and intricate little sketches of strange creatures. I flick through the pages again and again, but I can't focus on any one passage. The fact that I have this book in my hands is too big. I read snatches, tiny clues into what she was like when she was here, and each one is wondrous, but also devastating, because I never really knew her. I don't remember her voice, or her smell; I don't know how she looks when she is happy, or sad. Now, I guess I know a little bit. I know how she put words together, how she felt about someone called Ganymede and her potions for warding off the common cold.

It still isn't much. Most of the words are strangely obscured, they seem to blur when I look closely. After a while, I pull back from the book with a huff and tuck it into the pocket of my jacket. I shout out to Pa that I'm going for a walk. He calls back from his study, and I picture him at his old wooden desk, the narrow-faced brass clock ticking on the mantelpiece, his brow furrowed as he tries to read some tiny text without his glasses. And then I bang out of the front door and begin to prowl the winding streets of our ancient town, tucking my chin into my scarf as the cold November air flowers into my lungs. It's a thing I do, when I'm restless. I walk. Pa used to hate it: I think he worried I wouldn't come back. But I couldn't help myself, and I was never too late home, so he got used to it.

Tonight I head down into the very centre of town, where the cobbles of the market square are slick beneath my feet, and shadows cling beneath the old clock tower. The streets are narrow and twisty, and the sky overhead is star-spattered ink. I come here often. There's warmth in the streetlights, and the shabby, crenellated rooftops make me think of old Christmas cards. It's a small town, and most people know each other. They still talk about my mother, say how special she was. I smile and nod when they tell me, but it feels like a club I wasn't allowed into; I never got to see it for myself. I turn a corner, and the air whistles out of my chest.

Rising up behind the clock tower – taller, grander, shining like the moon itself – is the house. The one my mother sketched, with the balconies, and the tiny sparkling bridge, and the wide marble steps that sweep up to a massive, ornate porch. I take a step back, look around me wildly. Familiar rooftops spin over my head as I turn. I have walked these streets a thousand times. I know their nooks and crannies, and where they rise and fall. I know the way they smell in the morning, when the baker opens her shop, and in the evening, when the pubs are closing. I know that postbox on the corner, the bench beside it dedicated to *Mr A. Knowles*, who used to run the bookshop.

I collapse on to Mr Knowles's bench now and curl my fingers round the wooden slats. Take a breath of freezing air, and look up.

There is the house.

It was never there before.

3

The steps are smooth as glass, reflecting the lines of the house above. There's not a single smudge on them, not a winter-dried leaf, nothing. They loom over me, and I don't mean to be here at all, but I can't walk away now. What if I came back tomorrow and it was gone? What if it's only an illusion?

I tread on the first step, heartbeat thudding in my ears, just waiting for my foot to fall through, for this whole new world to collapse around me like some kind of dream. I hold my breath, bring my other foot up to join it and stand there for a long moment. It holds.

I look down. My boot is out of place, scuffed and muddy, and when I move up to the next step I can see that I've left a footprint. A real footprint, on a real step. A shudder rolls up my spine as I see that to either side of the steps the gardens have been left to grow wild, thick brambles winding up the dark branches of trees. If I slip or fall, I'll land in a tangle of thorns.

I keep going and it gets colder, until my breath is steaming and my knees are shaking. It seems to take hours, and all the time the wilderness to either side seems to be growing. There was a garden here once; my mother's sketch showed it clearly. There were flowers, in cultivated rows. They were loved.

I stumble when I get to the top – my head has been so full of the steps and the brambles that I forgot to look up as I was going. The porch opens up around me, built on pale marble pillars, every inch carved with flowers and trees and tiny winged figures that wink in the moonlight. The door is set back, sheltered from the elements. It's as wide as a car and made of stark white wood. I step forward, rest my hand against it, wondering if I dare to knock. The wood is soft and warm, and it gives slightly beneath my touch, like skin. I whip my hand away with a tiny shriek.

The door swings open.

I always thought I had a good imagination. When we played rounders at school, I'd be out in the field missing balls because in my mind I'd be riding on a starlit unicorn, or having a heroic battle with a storm giant about to lay siege to the town. I imagined what it would feel like to live in a world where fairies were real, to have a mother, to be popular like Jago.

Never in a thousand years could I have imagined a place like this. It isn't just the way it looks; it's the way it *breathes*. The air moves; it sings with the song of a thousand worlds: with snowglobes, each one churned up as if it's just been shaken. They ring out from their shelves, on either side of the enormous marble hallway stretching in front of me, and they swing from the ceiling on copper chains. They're small as bubbles at the top of the shelves, and nestled into heavy iron cradles at the bottom, full of feathers, glitter and flecks of gold falling over silent scenes trapped in glass. Bridges and mountains, sculpted domes and underwater caves, all half lost in a swirling tide, each with its own tiny human figure.

The door slams shut behind me, and a shadow flickers at the edge of my vision, twisting up a central staircase with curved banisters. The shudder I've been repressing worms its way up my spine. I ignore it and head for the stairs, moving carefully between the rows of gleaming globes. The air is musty, as if it hasn't been breathed enough, and there are cobwebs in all the corners, tangled around old, flickering chandeliers and snaking over picture rails.

I should leave. Right now. I turn on my heel and hover for a minute, two, three, looking from the door to the staircase. Then I think of my mother's sketch, and of the book in my pocket that is the closest I have ever come to her – except being here in this house, her house. The fact that I stumbled upon it tonight, after everything that's happened today, that must mean something. I grit my teeth and turn again, my boots squeaking on the polished marble floor, and head up the stairs.

The banister is smooth and worn. I imagine her coming up here, her hands where mine are now, her feet lingering on the same worn places. I wonder if she played hide and seek in all the empty spaces as a child. My eyes are on stalks for signs of her – photos, height marks on walls – but there aren't any. This is no ordinary house.

I already knew she was no ordinary person. Pa rarely speaks about her, and when he does, it's always from so far away. His mournful look chases every word until we're both desperate to drop it, but there were clues in all the things he told me. She crocheted scarves with silk, and then gave them away because she didn't need them. She laughed like a storybook witch, sang like a bird, shouted like a steam train – and nobody stood a chance against her when she set her mind to something. She rarely spoke about her family, or where she came from, but Pa knew there was magic there. It was bright and dark and full of hope, but there were other, more twisting things that gave her nightmares sometimes. She didn't use her magic around him, said it was best left behind, and that was what they argued about – he could see how much it cost her, not to breathe that air.

She didn't want *me* to breathe it either, but she left before I took my first steps, so she never got to tell me that herself. Pa told me she'd have worried, when he began to see traces of it in the things I did. He taught me to count through the moments when it got close, so that's what I've been doing. That's what I did this morning with Jago. I counted, and tried to pretend the magic – her magic – was all in my imagination.

Only it wasn't. Pa's been trying to tell me for a while that it would only grow, but I didn't want to hear it.

The stairs lead to a wide corridor where arched

windows look out on to narrow balconies and the tangled brambles of the neglected garden. Snowglobes hang from silver chains here, clustered together like small universes. I walk around them, watching as wild storms flurry within, and in a smaller, darker corridor, globes the size of a human head are set into alcoves in the walls. They glow strangely, ancient yellowed glass making rugged landscapes look ominous. A black iron staircase looms at one end of the corridor, a ghostly light filtering down.

Hurry.

I back up a couple of steps at the sound of small, hushed voices.

She'll find you. Be quick!

The room perches at the top of the house, beneath a huge dome roof that makes all the sounds echo. Stars wink overhead between smoky, shifting clouds, and it's hard to make out much detail in the miniature worlds that line the room on shelves of twisted metal. They flounder in swashing tides of bright whirling snow, black sands and deep blue seas that glimmer with tiny darting fish.

Who is it?

Is it her? Is it Ganymede?

No! 'Tis a new face, come to see us . . . and she has magic!

Run, you fool. You'll be lost as we are!

The ghost-like voices rustle and boom and fade to nothing. My skin prickles as I venture further into the room. There is danger here. I don't know where it comes from, that sense, but it's as real as the taste of copper in my mouth. I peer into the nearest globe to find a solitary tree, its golden leaves in a great mound at the base of its trunk. They swirl up as I watch, so I move on to another: a half-ruined lighthouse perched on the edge of a cliff, beads of ice gathered in every crevice. The next is a circus top with a single tiger prowling around its perimeter. I stare at that one until the tiger lifts its head and roars at me, tiny stars whooshing up around its paws.

Clementine?

I follow the sound and see a boy at the bottom of a steep, snow-covered hill, one hand resting on the side of an enormous golden dog. The dog whines as I get closer, and the boy turns to it, soothing it with mumbled words.

'Was that you?' I ask, wincing as my hushed voice ricochets around the glass-domed roof.

23

The boy turns back to face me.

Don't you recognize me?

I stare at him for long minutes, wracking my brain. It's hard to see clearly through the glass, and his features are so tiny.

'Who are you?'

Dylan.

Snow falls harder all around him as he stares at me, a strange half-hope in his dark eyes. He curls his hand deeper into the dog's coat, and he shivers.

And then I know him.

Dylan, who helped me up after the netball smacked like ice into the side of my face. Dylan, who shivered beside me at the bus stop on so many bitter mornings. Who talked to me, but only when it suited him. Only when his best friend, Jago, wasn't in sight.

Dylan, who was sitting beside Jago earlier today, watching silently as he poked me in the small of my back.

4

What are you doing here?

I watch him for a long time, trying to convince the logical part of my mind that it really is him, miniaturized in a snowglobe. He steps closer to the glass, leaving the dog to wander over thin grass that pokes through the snow, and puts his hands against it.

Clementine, is that really you?

He sounds desperate, not like the Dylan I know, who's quick to smile, and easy with words. He tricks me every day – says 'hi', picks up my bag when it goes sliding across the bus floor – then we get through those green gates, and he gives me a wave and goes about his day with Jago, not even meeting my eye.

How did he end up here?

Please tell me you can hear me, he whispers.

'I can hear you.'

He stares at me for a long moment then presses his forehead against the glass.

'Dylan?'

How long has it been?

I perch on the arm of one of the old chairs, so my eyes are on a level with the globe. The material is frayed and bobbly; I rub my palms into it until it hurts. Just so I know this is real.

How long, since I was out there? He looks up, clenches his hands into fists, as if he'll pound at the glass. As if that's just what he's been doing all this time.

'I saw you today.'

Have they stopped looking? How long has it been, Clem?

'It was today, Dylan! I saw you at school this morning!'

It was a lifetime ago! he shouts, striking at the glass between us.

When he's finished pounding and he's sitting on the frozen ground, I ask, 'What happened?' The dog shuffles around him, nudging against his neck every so often. 'How did you end up in there?'

He doesn't say anything. He puts his hand up to the

dog and hooks his fingers into its coat, hauling himself up. I've never seen anybody look so weary.

'Dylan? How do I get you out? What *happened*?'

I don't know. I was walking along the street. It was misty, and it got colder and colder, and then there was a hill . . . and I was here.

'With the dog?'

Helios. He came after. I don't know how it works. He just appeared one day.

'One day? But you've only been here one day, Dylan.'

No, he says. *I don't know how long it's been, but it isn't just a day. Weeks, or months – I can feel the time passing, but I can't tell properly because there's no night here. The sky doesn't change, except when the storms come.*

He leans into Helios with another shiver, and stares at me. The hill rises behind him, snow shifting along its surface as the wind blows. On the top of the slope is a mean little house made of weathered wood with a tiny window at the top and a huge stable door at the bottom. There's nothing comforting about it.

'Is that where you live?'

I've tried to reach the house, but the hill is too steep, too icy. I can't get up there.

27

Snow begins to fall, and he tucks his chin into his jacket as it gathers in his brown hair, catching on his eyebrows.

Are you really here? he asks, his voice muffled.

I nod. 'I'll get you out.'

He shakes his head. And then his face darkens, and the globes around him begin to swirl. The snow falls harder, Helios barks and then silence. Utter stillness, all around, Dylan and Helios frozen into position, his face turned from mine so I can't see his expression.

A bony hand claps on to my shoulder.

'What are you doing here?' asks a dry voice that sounds as if it hasn't spoken for a thousand years. 'Turn, child, let me see you. How did you get in?'

I swallow and turn, the hand still on my shoulder. Against the pale starlight of the room, she is a shadow, a collection of shapes that makes no sense.

'Light,' she snaps, drawing away from me, her voice swelling and filling the room. The globes begin to glow, their light a silver haze that grows until the shadows are gone.

We stare at each other for the longest, strangest time. She is tall and angular, her features softened only by an enormous mane of silver hair, some of it matted, some of it plaited, some of it twisted into a bun on top of her head. Her long robe seems to be a collection of materials she threw together in a hurry: lace trails from the sleeves, the pewter bodice looks almost like armour and the collar is made of pale, speckled feathers. The air around her vibrates, as though she's in the centre of a heat haze. She's unearthly, beautiful, alien and thoroughly chilling.

Ganymede! scream the voices from the snowglobes.

'Who are you?' I whisper. Who is Ganymede, and what does she have to do with my mother? There must be a link; her name was in my mother's book, and this is the house my mother drew. This place rings with the magic that I've been denying for so long.

'Who am *I*?' she shrieks. 'Who are *you*?'

Run, run, run, RUN!

The air simmers between us, and her fingers twitch as her eyes narrow; any moment now she's going to grab me again.

RUN!

I run and I don't look back. I don't linger on the globes I pass, though tiny figures put their hands up against the glass as avalanches thunder around them, though the whole house seems to rumble with my footsteps.

I just run.

5

This is a mistake. I skitter down the marble steps, already knowing it's the wrong thing to do. By the time I hit the path, my stomach is churning, not because of everything that's just happened, but because I'm running away. I could at least have grabbed Dylan's snowglobe.

I never even thought of it.

I linger by the twisted iron gate, my back to the house, my mind a scramble of snowglobes and tiny whirling storms, and that woman Ganymede's silver eyes, staring right into my heart as if she already knows everything inside me.

What if I turn round now and the house isn't there any more? What if I just cursed Dylan to years longer living like that? He's two-faced, and sometimes I think

31

that's worse than just plain mean, because it plays tricks on you. But, whatever he is, he doesn't deserve this. He doesn't deserve to be abandoned there by me.

I steel myself and turn to go back in, but the door bangs open and a thousand voices roar out:

RUN!

Pa is pacing the hallway when I get in. My whole body is shaking, wired with adrenaline.

'Clem! Where have you been?'

'I was walking. Sorry.'

He looks me up and down, and I obviously look pretty awful, because he doesn't say anything else. He just strides off to the kitchen and calls me in after him. I loiter in the hallway, taking my jacket off, flicking through the pages of the book, hoping to see a page usefully labelled 'Snowglobes and How to Break Them'.

I have to go back – I've been chanting it to myself the whole way home. I need to get him out of there. I'll read the book and figure out how to protect myself against Ganymede, whoever she is, and then I'll go back in there. I imagine it: moonlight striking through the glass dome as I liberate him; Ganymede standing powerless before my magical powers. I picture myself like an energy ball, strobes cutting through the air as we escape, and it's not so different from all the fantasies I've built in my mind over the years, except this time it's real, and I'm already cross with myself because when it came to it I wasn't as brave as I thought I would be.

'Clem!'

'Coming!' I tuck the book into my back pocket and trail into the kitchen.

Pa scrambles eggs, toasts bread. Shoves the plate over to me.

'Aren't you having any?'

'I already ate,' he says. He stares at me while I eat. 'Clem . . .'

'Hmm?'

But he can't find the words. He just looks at me sadly.

'What?'

'Just . . . don't get lost.'

I look down at the empty plate. He knows things are going on. Maybe he knows more than I do. Why is it so hard to ask? Why don't I just say, 'Oh, hey, I discovered this house today, and you'll never guess who was in it, trapped in a *snowglobe* . . . !'

'Pa?'

But he's already gone. I missed the moment.

I cannot sleep. I don't know why I'm even trying. I should just get up and go back there right now, except Pa is a light sleeper, so I'll have to wait until morning. But I've never felt guilt like this; it's like a rock on my chest. I reach down under the bed for my head torch and shove it on, grabbing my mother's book. I'll just read a couple more pages. My eyes flick over the words and it's hard to focus, but eventually, fair sparking with frustration, I find a page where the writing is smoother, more evenly spaced. The passage is boldly entitled 'MAGIC', and that seems as good a place to start as any.

In reality, our magic is not so much the spell-saying or anything formal like that. It is a connection with the world; with the growing of new life, or the shaping of metals; with the moon and the sun (Ganymede is the moon, I have always thought, and Io the sun, and I . . . perhaps the earth?). Ganymede says I dream too much and should take our work more seriously. I do not think that magic ought always to be serious. It is such fun! It is full of colour and life! My sisters do not see it the same way, I suppose. For them, it is always the pull of power and control, of responsibility.

Our parents trained them well in that, especially Gan. She has a way with the globes that made Papa glow with pride. One look of her sharp silver eyes, one click of her fingers, and those marauding magicians are caught up and trapped in their little glass cells. I am not sure it is right, to trap all *things magical. I would like to leave this place, to venture further and find the magic that is still out there in the real world, but my sisters are welded here, their roots deep within the walls of the house. Io sees no interest in the outside world, she calls it grey and dull, and Ganymede would rather hide from it all. She can hide the whole house!*

Ganymede is my mother's sister! It shouldn't be a surprise that I'm related to such an odd creature, and yet it doesn't feel comfortable at all. That house raises so many questions, and I ran away, just like my mother did. All those years of planning my bravery, and, when it came down to it, I ran.

I can go back. If Ganymede and my mother have magic, then so do I, and there must be a way to help

Dylan. I think back to this morning, which seems like years ago already, and the feeling that came over me before I knocked Jago across the room, that feeling that changed everything. It had been building up for so long – I counted and counted, and he poked and poked, until my blood was roaring. I turn the head torch off.

One, two, three, four . . .

This is not how Pa imagined me using his counting trick.

Seven, eight, nine . . .

I shove my hand out into the darkness. Nothing.

Forty, forty-one . . . fifty-six . . .

I thrust again, and a tiny wire of amber spirals between my thumb and my index finger.

Yep, I'm weird. I grin as the room lights up.

That's magic. Real, actual magic, done by me.

A door bangs and I'm awake, dreams of lost boys and orange sparks still alive in my mind. It's almost surprising to find myself in my same old bedroom, with all my same old stuff; it takes me a while to work out that it was the front door that woke me. It's only just dawn, but Pa is always out with first light, even in midsummer when it's barely five. Sometimes I used to watch him go. He seemed a little bit magical himself then as he trod light-footed in the shadows, head high, hair blazing, birds singing all around as the sky started to lighten.

I pull myself up and peer out of the window now, watching him disappear out of sight. Not so much magical, more like elusive and distracted. He says he does it to get to the university fresh and early, before anybody else is there to bother him. It's his routine. Even at weekends, off he goes at full charge. I have wondered, sometimes, if it's to get away from me, if I remind him so much of Mum that he can't bear to look at me too much. Now I wonder if he's still searching for her.

Maybe he never stopped thinking of her. I know the rest of the town hasn't; they loved the ground she walked on, and they still do. All the shopkeepers, Mrs Pick the librarian, the lollipop man, all of them have stories to tell about her contagious wicked laughter, the way birds gathered in the trees when she was near, the way her song rippled through the streets and made the day shine brighter. The way they tell it, she became the heart of the whole place.

And then she left us all.

The white house flashes in front of my eyes. That's where the answers are. I pull myself out of bed, shove my clothes on and rush out of the flat with a biscuit in my mouth and the book in my jacket pocket. I race past the bus stop where Dylan and I saw each other just yesterday and run down all the familiar streets, jumping down the worn old stone steps by the church. My heart is racing, it's *singing* with wanting to get into that house and get Dylan out of there.

I skid round the corner, breath bursting out.

The house isn't there.

6

I cannot sleep.

I've suffered this for so long: dreamless slumber, broken only by waking to this living nightmare that's impossible to understand. How did I get here? How is it possible to be trapped in glass? The sky overhead is an unchanging solid mass of pale grey; behind me, the hill with that forsaken house. If I stare beyond the glass at a particular angle, there's a whole different reality: a vast room full of shelves where worlds as bleak as mine are stacked.

Sometimes Io stalks through this place, bringing her storms with her, so that I cannot stand straight. Sometimes in the sky of that larger world out there, where Ganymede wears her loneliness like a second skin, I can see stars. For a while, I wished on them: I wished for school, I wished for home, I wished for the most boring things I could think of. I would do homework for a hundred years just to be able to eat toast while I did it, and I would never use magic again. Not ever.

I stopped wishing a long time ago. Stopped thinking, remembering, stopped the bargaining. Then the dog came. I'd never so much as stroked a dog before, and for a while we skirted around each other. And then he moved closer. He snorted his breath into my face, and it stank, and it was real – it was warm. I called him Helios because it means 'the sun', and I leaned into him, and he was really, truly there. We spend our moments together now, facing this way or that. Sometimes we try to climb the hill. Sometimes I howl, and sometimes he barks, but that's OK, because we understand each other.

Now we are thrown into chaos, and we can't rest, because Clementine was here. Of all the people, Clementine. How can I ask her for help?

I should have said sorry. Sorry I didn't stop him. Sorry I hid behind Jago, watching while the magic we both have danced in her eyes, while I buried mine deep down so nobody would ever know.

But I didn't. I didn't even think of it. And now she's gone, and I don't know if she'll ever come back again. Why would she come back into this place and risk everything, for me?

7

'No,' I whisper.

NO!

It isn't there. I approach the same spot from every angle, walk around in circles, look for it out of the corner of my eye, run at it as if I can surprise it into being. But the place where the house stood is just an old, dilapidated park. I pace for hours and then slump on to the bench, curling the book in my hand, staring into emptiness until my eyes water, until my bum is numb with cold and my feet have lost all their feeling. I've checked to see if my mother wrote anything about seeing through Ganymede's hiding spell, but there was nothing; I could barely see straight. I call on every emotion I've ever felt, hoping to awaken some sort of magic that will reveal the house to me, flex my fingers to see if I can make a spark, but nothing happens, and all the time I'm calling to Dylan in my mind, hoping just maybe he'll hear me.

I came back! Dylan!

Nothing. Not a glimmer of marble, not a spark, or a wink of anything resembling that bewitching place.

Was it a dream?

'Clementine?'

I start, looking up to see Pa coming towards me, a frown on his face.

'What are you doing sitting here in the cold?'

'I needed some air. What are *you* doing here?'

He looks from me to the playground, his eyes a bit wild. 'I was heading home to make us some lunch. Why are you *here*, though? Did you see something?'

'I thought I did, yesterday.'

'What was it, Clem? Do you see it now?' He steps closer to the old iron railings, puts his hand on the cold metal.

It wasn't a dream. He knows about the house.

'It's gone,' I say heavily, staring at him as old memories stir in my mind. Memories of coming here with him in the early morning, when I was small. Of sitting on this very bench eating pastries, while the sun made the rooftops gleam. Has he really just been waiting for her this whole time?

'Pa . . .'

'You saw the house?' He looks back to me, his tired brown eyes gleaming. 'Did you see it? Did you go in, Clem? Was anybody there?'

'Like who?'

'It was your mother's house. She was living there with her sisters when I met her . . . What did you see, Clem?' He comes and perches next to me on the bench, his eyes still flitting from me to the place where the house was before. 'Tell me everything.'

'There were thousands of snowglobes,' I say. 'They were all whirling; the house was full of them. It was cold, and bright, and it smelt of dust . . . and I ran away, before I should have. And I came back, but now it's gone.'

'This is where I first saw her, here, at dawn, when all the birds were singing,' he says, staring at the hard packed earth of the old park, the scrubby grass, the rusted metal slide. 'I was restless, walking, and there she was, in the most incredible garden . . .' He looks at me. 'Did you see the garden?'

'Yes.' I don't tell him that it's a ruin now, all shadows and thorns.

43

'And you went in?' He frowns. 'It wasn't wise, Clem. You can't just go wandering into strange old houses. It's a dangerous place.'

'I got out again,' I say. 'And now I can't even see it, so it's not too much of a danger, is it?' I can't help the snap in my voice. I've wondered about my mother for a lifetime. We talked about her magic, all the joy she brought, and I knew she was special, but I never knew about a magical hiding *house*. He never told me she had sisters. And now it's all gone again, before I even had a chance to find out more.

'Let's go home,' he says, his face tightening.

He stands and looks down at me, and I fold my arms, feeling all small and prickly.

'I don't want to.'

'Pardon?'

'I'm going to stay here until it's back. I want to go in again.'

'No you're not,' he says, his tone hardening. 'You look like you've been here all morning; you're nearly blue with cold. Get up, Clem. I'm not leaving you here.'

He starts to walk away, as if I'm just going to follow, as if it isn't even a question.

'I met Ganymede!' I shout after him, standing up.

He turns, his face drained of colour.

'What?'

'Yep. I met her.' I fold my arms. 'My *aunt*.'

'What were you thinking, going into that place all alone?' he shouts after an awful moment of silence, only broken by the sound of shop awnings being opened for the day. I can smell fresh bread, hear the rumble of a bus engine in the distance. My stomach sours as he glares at me. I've never seen him in such a temper. 'And now you're back for more? You have no idea what you're walking into, Clem. I forbid this! Home, now!' He gestures in the vague direction of our flat, his breath steaming in the bitter air.

'No! You can't forbid me! Don't you want me to find out what happened? I know you never stopped looking for her, Pa!' My face is hot, my hands shaking – I don't know what's happening. We don't fall out, me and my pa; we're all we have. We laugh together at old films, we make our own popcorn and on Sundays we go for brunch at the old cafe on the bridge, and watch people pass by out of the wide, dusty windows. We don't shout at each other in the street. Except today we do. Today we stand and glare at each other, arms folded, and my heart is hammering so hard I can hardly see straight.

'I am not discussing this here,' he says finally, his eyes flicking to the empty space where we both know the house still stands. 'Walk home with me, and we can talk.' He takes a deep breath. 'Please, Clementine. Now.'

He isn't going to leave without me. And while he's here the house isn't going to appear. It's clear it's been hiding from him all this time. Ganymede has been hiding it from him. Maybe it was *my* magic that broke through her spell yesterday. Maybe she's hiding it even harder now.

'OK,' I whisper.

I'LL BE BACK! I shout it as loud as I can in my mind, just hoping Dylan will hear me. Because, whatever Pa says, this is not where this ends.

I am only just beginning.

'I'm sorry for shouting,' Pa says in a low voice as soon as we're away from the square. 'I know you need answers, but I don't think that's the place to find them.' He glances at me.

The low sun flashes through the gaps between buildings and makes my eyes burn.

'I don't know why she didn't come back that day. We had an argument, but it was nothing; we were just tired. We'd run out of milk –' he sighs – 'and she went out to get some air, and she just didn't come home. I always wondered if she'd gone back to the house, if something had happened there, but I couldn't find it. It just wasn't there. It's been a long time now, Clem, and your mother was a powerful, resourceful woman. If she'd wanted to be found, I'd have found her.'

It sounds more like a question than a statement. He doesn't know anything, I realize. He couldn't find her himself, and now he wants to stop me, just when there's a chance.

'So, what, I'm not even supposed to look? You want me just to forget about it?'

'Yes! Yes, that's what I want.' He stops, puts his hands on my shoulders. 'You have magic, Clem; we both knew you'd have it. And I know it hurts, that there are no clear answers; I know you lost her just as much as I did, maybe even more. But there are no good things in that house! Your mother left it for a reason, and I don't trust anything you might find there. We'll find our way together. I'll help you. There must be more books – we can learn about your magic so that you can manage it. But you cannot go back there. Ganymede is dangerous – the whole place is.'

'But she's my *aunt*, isn't she? So I can talk to her . . .'

'No,' he says, moving back. 'No, you mustn't. She may be your aunt, but who knows what she is capable of? Your mother never even told them she'd had a child. She wanted to protect you from it all, and that's what I'll do, Clem, till my dying day. If Ganymede is drawing you here . . . we should have moved away. I won't lose *you* to that place too.' His face darkens. 'Come on –' he storms ahead – 'lunch. And I'll think about what we're going to do next.'

I have a thousand retorts on my tongue, and a thousand more questions, but they're all wedged deep inside me. I force my feet after his, my mind whirring. Magic, and school suspension, the book and the house. Dylan in a globe. Now Pa seems to be saying we should move somewhere else, just to get away from the house.

That's not happening.

He's wrong about it all. He thinks there's a way for me to just walk away. He doesn't know about Dylan, or all the magicians trapped in there. He doesn't know that the one promise I've made to myself is that I would never just abandon the people who need me most.

Never.

He keeps darting me concerned looks, so I hold my chin up and try to keep the fire out of my eyes, but already I am scheming. Already I am halfway there.

Lunch is all silence and swallowing, the crusts on the bread are too hard, and I feel cold. Everything is different, and I can hardly look at Pa, who paces and frets because he has to go back to work after lunch.

'We can talk more –' he kisses the top of my head while I push cheese gratings around my plate – 'when I'm home later. We can order Chinese, and we can talk all night, Clem, but you have to promise you won't go back there. Not today, not until we've talked. Can you promise?'

I promise with my fingers crossed, and my blood prickles in my veins when I do it, so I know just how wrong it is, but I do it anyway. My mouth is dry, and our smiles are thin, and it's a relief when he's gone. I clear the table, clean it until it shines, and get my mother's book out again, studying the sketch and trying to build a solid picture in my mind, hoping that will help when I get there. I do a bit of hoovering and leave the vacuum cleaner poking out of the cupboard so Pa can tell, squirt a bit of polish about, and upend a folder of paper over my bed so it looks like I've been studying.

And then I head out, leaving a note for Pa, telling him I'm going to catch up on schoolwork with Lizzie, that I'll be back by nine, and we can talk then.

Lizzie was my best friend at primary school. We don't see each other any more; she has new friends now. Pa doesn't know that bit. We were pretty good together once, before it all went wrong.

It was the summer before we started secondary school, my eleventh birthday. She came over to watch films and eat pizza, but the film was about this mother and daughter, and the mother died, and when the daughter cried, so did I, and Lizzie moved closer and put her arm round me. But when she looked closer,she turned pale and scrambled away from me.

'What is it?' I asked, wiping tears from my cheeks with my fingers.

'Your eyes!'

I stood up, looked in the mirror. My brown irises were flickering, flashing shards of amber.

'I have to go,' she said, but I hardly heard her – my heart was hammering too loud.

And we never spoke after that; I don't think either of us knew what to say. Pa said it would be OK. He taught me to count when the feeling flared, and I told myself it was just a one-time thing. I never felt it happen again.

Jago saw it somehow, though. On that first day, when he said my eyes were weird, I'd rushed to the loo to check. They were fine, but he'd seen something there. Maybe just a flash. I counted harder after that.

Anyway, I don't go to Lizzie's house – I haven't been there for over a year. Instead I head back into town, walking slower this time, as if I can creep up on it. It's dusk, but the moon is nowhere to be seen, and clouds sit heavy over the town. I start down the winding street towards the bakery and the bench, and snow starts to fall, which feels like hope, somehow. I look at the ground and watch the icy flakes dissolve into the gaps between cobbles and wish as hard as I can, *please*, until static makes my hair fly up around my head. Then I look up, and my heart sings, because it's here, looming over me, white as milk, almost glowing against the gloom, the tower cutting through the clouds.

I clench my fists and stride out across the square, and I never take my eyes off it, not for an instant. I just keep going: through the gate, up the steps, past all the tangled vines and clutching branches. I plant my feet firm and I charge up until I'm at the wide door that feels like warm skin. I brace myself, spread my hands and push against it.

The door swings open. Holding my breath, I step through and close it behind me, my eyes searching the spinning air for my moth-whirl of an aunt. There is no sign, and, for now, the shadowed corners are still, the worlds around me at rest.

Clementine?

Dylan's voice is thin, desperate.

I'm coming, I whisper inwardly, hoping Ganymede won't hear my thoughts. But as soon as the words have bloomed in my mind storms start to swirl in the globes, tiny golden stars flashing as they tumble over a darkened village, snow falling over mountains. Pale bone-like castles swim in seas of glitter, bright blossoms scatter over crooked clock towers. A young woman sits on church steps in one globe, her face turned to the sky, and in another there's an acrobat in a silver suit on top of the tallest needle tower, hands together as if he's about to jump.

I rush to the stairs, sliding one hand up the pale banister as I run as fast as I can to the top, and down the first corridor. My ears feel stretched with listening for her, my skin tight with goosebumps. And then the globes in the alcoves of the wall begin to glow, and the air thickens around me.

I turn slowly, my belly a pit of snakes.

Ganymede is here.

'You!' she says, coming at me down the corridor fast as smoke, a wolfish snarl on her bony face. 'I don't know how you keep getting in here, but you won't leave so easily this time.'

She raises an arm and there's a silvery, shivering sound that rings through the house. Dust and tiny flakes of plaster rain down over our heads, a cold mist swirls between us, and by the time I can see clearly the grand staircase has vanished. Ganymede looms over me, and there's no way back.

8

'Speechless?' she whispers. 'Cat got your tongue? Not my Portia, surely – *Portia!*' A white cat comes bounding down the corridor, green eyes like cold fire, and Ganymede acknowledges her with a nod. 'Show me now – do you have our mystery girl's tongue? Open up!'

The cat opens a pink mouth to meow loudly.

'It doesn't *seem* to be in there,' Ganymede says.

The cat meows again, and I swear I can almost hear the footsteps of a hundred mice fleeing from that sound. The green eyes blink at me, the tail curls in a question mark and then Portia bounds up on to the nearest windowsill and settles down to sleep. Ganymede looks back at me.

'Explain yourself,' she says, her tone like an iron trap.

'Why are you here? How did you get past my wards and all the traps I laid?'

'I didn't notice any,' I say, steeling myself. 'Perhaps you forgot.'

She steps back, her eyebrows swooping up. 'So you dare to speak? You dare to speak, and to *cheek* me? What is this? Who are you?'

'Clementine.'

She looks me up and down. 'You most certainly are not a small orange fruit! IMPERTINENCE! Now tell me this instant, what business do you have here? *Years* and none dared disturb my peace: a *thousand* nights of solitude, broken by nothing but the song of the moon. It was delicious, it was a melodious clamour of nothing, and now there is YOU! Why have you come back here?'

'My *name* is Clementine.'

She frowns. 'There are many moons you could be named for, why did your parents choose fruit? To go with your hair?' She pauses, a wrinkle appearing between her brows as she stares at my hair. 'WHO is your mother?' She whips out suddenly, lunging in close as if to smell me, making all the hairs on my arms stand up. 'I know that fiery hair.'

'M-my . . .'

'Callisto? Is my Callisto your mother?' She circles me, her skirts rustling as she goes. 'Are you hers? DON'T stand there gaping at me, child!'

'Callie,' I breathe, utterly distracted by her moth-like fluttering all about in my face, lace and tatters flying. 'Pa said she was called Callie.'

'*Callie?*' Tears stand in her dark eyes. 'What is Callie? Of what moon does that tally? Do you mean *Callisto*? She was my most beloved heart. But . . . I didn't know she had a child. She can't have had a child!' She looks me up and down, her hands shaking as she reaches out, and then she stops herself. The lights around us flicker before going out and, in the new darkness, shadows spiral down her face in fine lines. 'I would have known!'

'Who *are* you?' I ask in a whisper. Can this creature really be related to me? She barely seems human at all.

'I am Ganymede,' she says, still staring at me. 'Ganymede the eldest, and then there was bright Io, and then our youngest, Callisto. We lived here together for many years before my solitude began. But what do you know of all of this? How did you find me?'

'I-I don't know . . .' I stammer. 'I didn't know about

this house until yesterday. My mother left when I was small. She left a book, and this house was in it . . .'

'Do you mean her diary? But why wouldn't she tell me, if she'd had a child?' Ganymede mutters again, looking up at the snowglobes that hang from the ceiling on slender coils of golden wire. She taps at one with a long finger and it begins to whirl, a tiny storm of steel beads over a narrow, spindly bridge, a tiny man clinging to the struts. 'We are sisters; we trusted each other with everything!' She frowns. 'How old are you, child?'

'Twelve.'

'All this time!' She steps closer, her eyes gleaming. 'Where have you been? If you are hers, why would she hide you from us?'

'I was with my pa. He told me she left, but he never knew why. Do you know what happened?'

Something flashes across her face, but she quickly recovers herself. 'I can't help you,' she says. 'I don't even know who you are.'

'I'm Callisto's daughter! Pa gave me her book, and this morning he told me to never come back because you're dangerous, but here I am.'

'Yes,' she says. 'So you are. And you have disobeyed, which is something your mother would have done. *If* this is all to be believed. You have a book, you say – let me see it.' She stoops towards me, her spine curving like a great iron hook.

Clementine!

Dylan. I cling to his voice; that's why I came back. Never mind Ganymede. Never mind anything else. I came to get Dylan out of his prison and back home.

Ganymede screeches as I turn and run down the corridor. The marble walls shudder and the globes shift on their shelves, glass tinkling all around me; worlds sliding, falling, smashing into each other. I look over my shoulder as I skitter round a corner, and she is hurrying after me, her face taut with concentration, globes all around her slowly righting themselves, not a single one broken. She moves faster and faster, shadows boiling in the air around her, and I run harder, pulling globes off shelves as I go to keep her busy. I don't know what I'll do when I get to the attic, but Dylan is there, so I keep going anyway, up the iron staircase, calling for him – '*DYLAN!*'

A flash of something goes through me as I put him at the centre of my mind, and when I skid into the room, the carpet crunches like snow beneath my feet. It *is* snow beneath my feet. Snow in my eyes, and my mouth;

snow pelting into my face on a bitter, sweeping wind. There is no attic room here. There are no snowglobes. There is no carpet. No domed windows – just snow. I take a step, stretching my arms out for balance, and immediately slip on ice, skidding down a slope and colliding with a small wooden hut.

I burrow my face into my jacket and put one hand out to the rough, cold wood, hauling myself up and staggering around until I find the door. It opens with a creak, and I brace myself as I go in, wondering what I'm going to find next.

It's just an empty room, with bare walls and little snow drifts on the floor where there are gaps between the wooden boards. There's nothing here, and yet as I stand in the middle, shivering and trying to work out what just happened, the room starts to change.

First, a rug appears on the floor, brightly striped and just like the one in my room at home. I step on to it. When I look up, there is a chandelier swinging from the ceiling, looking very much like one of those in Ganymede's house. I blink, and when I open my eyes, the walls are covered in blue paper, with pictures of my pa and me hanging over a tiny wrought-iron fireplace like the one in our sitting room. Even the shining red tiles on the hearth are the same. I step closer to one of the pictures and there's me, there's Pa, and there's a smudged shape beside him. The place my mother might be, if I knew what she looked like.

It's all an illusion. It must be. It's what this place would be, if I lived here. *If I used my magic to make it a home.* The thought thunders at me, and the walls shake as I begin to understand. Of course, I'm in a globe! When I ran from Ganymede, I must have somehow used my magic to pull me through, to get me to Dylan.

Dylan's globe, with the little wooden house.

I wrench open the little door and stumble out into a whirling white storm.

'Dylan?' I shout. The door slams shut behind me and I start down the slope keeping the house at my back. When I saw him last time, he was at the bottom, and the house was at the top. I don't know how I ended up in here, but if I'm inside the globe, he must be here somewhere.

Mustn't he?

'DYLAN!'

It's impossible to see. I just keep sliding my feet forward, slithering and scrambling, down and down, over snow-covered rock ledges and patches of sheer ice, until the way gets steeper and I lose my footing entirely, careering down the rest of the hill on my backside and landing in a heap at the bottom, an invisible barrier preventing me going any further.

'Clementine?'

I turn to look at the boy *I* was supposed to be rescuing.

'Dylan!'

He stoops down to me, his face pinched with cold. He looks thin and tired, an echo of the boy I saw at school yesterday. What has happened to him here in that short time?

'What are you doing here?' he whispers. 'How did you get in?'

I look around. It's hard to breathe in the icy air. I get to my knees and tuck my freezing hands into my armpits. 'I don't know. I was in the house with Ganymede, she was chasing me, and I ended up in that little house!'

'The house up there?' He squints as he looks up the hill; it's barely visible in the mist of fine snow. 'How did you do that? What did you do?'

'I don't know . . .' My voice trails off. 'She's terrifying. I was running to get you, and she was coming after me, and I ended up here. How *did* that happen?' I look around, but there's not much to see: a dull grey sky, still showering us with snow, and the solitary icy hill, the matchstick house just a smudge of brown overhead. No pathways. No tracks but our own. 'What do we do now?'

He stares down at me, his eyes bloodshot and bleary. Of course he doesn't have the answers; I was supposed to be the one rescuing him. Now we're both stuck in his snowglobe, and whatever magic I had in me just a moment ago has fled, leaving me light-headed.

9

'Get up,' Dylan says, pulling me out of the snow.

A storm is building, dark clouds swell on the horizon, and a fierce, bitter wind is blowing. My cheeks sting with cold, and my feet are like blocks of ice.

'Hold on to Helios, keep moving.' He pulls me to the huge dog and tucks one of his hands deep into his golden coat, gesturing for me to do the same. Helios looks at me over his shoulder and huffs, but he doesn't move away. His fur is wiry, his body warm and firm as a rock between us.

'What are we going to do?' I whisper, trying not to let my teeth chatter. 'I meant to get you out, not put myself *in*!'

He stares at me.

'Maybe it's a dream,' he mutters to himself. 'You're

not really here. That's what it is. You're an illusion.' He searches me over with haunted eyes. 'Just one of Io's tricks.'

'I'm not a trick!'

'How can I know that?'

'I know things.' I search my mind for the right thing to say as he stares unblinking. 'Your best friend is Jago. You and I talk on the bus to school. You're kind, sometimes . . .'

'I watched,' he says. 'Jago was mean, and I didn't stop him. But that was a long time ago, and none of it means anything now.' He sighs and leans into Helios. 'If you're not a trick, you must be my subconscious, because I've been in here too long and I'm losing my mind.'

'No,' I say. 'You're not. You've been here for a day, that's all, however long it might seem to you. And now I'm here with you, so you could at least look a bit happy about that! Look, Helios can see me. Can't you, boy?' I wheedle and smile, but Helios refuses to look at me, which doesn't help. 'I swear, Dylan, I'm really here. We just need to find our way out!'

'Out of here?' He shakes his head. 'There is no way out.'

'Well, I got in, so it must be possible!' I turn from

him and try to stir the magic I used to get in here, the magic that made the mean little house a home, but the spark has gone, for now at least. 'How did *you* end up in here, anyway?'

He mutters something under his breath.

'What?'

'I don't know,' he says. 'And you didn't really get in, because you're not really here. Only Io can get in and out, and you're just an illusion sent by her!' His eyes flicker, and suddenly he rushes at me, knocking me to the ground.

'Dylan!' I shout, pushing him off me and rolling out of his way. He stands up, looming over me. 'Why did you do that?'

'You're not real; you can't be real,' he whispers, staring, staring at me all the time. 'Are you a dream?' He pinches his arm, and I notice there's a row of small bruises on the inside of his wrist where he's clearly done it countless times before.

'Stop that!' I reach out and grab his wrist just as a bitter wind starts to howl around us. Snow blows into our faces, the flakes small and hard as ice.

Dylan looks down at my hand.

'You're warm,' he whispers. His eyes widen, and he

looks me up and down. 'Is it really you?'

'It's really me,' I say. 'I promise, Dylan. It's me. I'm so sorry I didn't get you out the first time I found the house. I was so shocked, and Ganymede was there . . . I came back, though. I came back to get you out!'

'You got in by yourself? Can't you get us out the same way?'

'I don't know how! I didn't mean to get in – it just happened . . .'

'Make it just happen again, then!'

I close my eyes, partly to escape his intensity, and try to see Ganymede's house, to will us back there somehow, but the images flicker and falter. I can't grab hold of anything.

'I can't,' I say eventually.

'We need to move,' he says after a long, pained silence, as the wind howls and the snow beneath our feet starts to shift along the ground. 'Don't stand there like a flag – you'll get the full force of it. Come on.' He starts down the icy rocks and, with a quick look at the sky, darts round to the right, gesturing for me to follow him.

'Why don't we try the house?' I ask. 'At least we'd be out of the wind.'

'I can't get up the hill,' he says. 'I've tried; it's too steep.'

'We could try it together . . .' I stare up the hill. It looks impossible, and my magic is a damp curl in the base of my stomach, good for nothing right now.

'Forget the house!' Dylan says. 'Just keep your head down – there's no time now.'

We crouch with the hill at our backs, and Helios sits on our feet, as the wind picks up, and the snow flies tornado-fast over our heads, until it feels like the whole world has turned upside down. I make myself as small as I can, my face tucked hard against my knees, and the storm beats all around us with a shuddering, booming roar. And in the midst of it all darkness falls, quick as a light being turned off. It's not like falling asleep; it's like being turned to stone. I can hear my heartbeat, feel my hair streaming in the wind, my aching legs, but I can't move. I can't speak. I start to panic, but a warm shoulder wedges hard against my own and, though I can't see it, I can picture him, sitting by me. I can feel the warmth of Helios at my feet.

When the storm has passed, I still can't move. I still can't speak. I just stare at Dylan. It's horrifying. No shelter, no comfort. Just being thrown around at someone else's whim, turned to a static figure in a globe, unable to do anything about it. Was it Io, or Ganymede, stalking through the attic room? Will she discover us in here together, and do something even worse to us?

'Dylan . . .'

'Give it a minute,' he says in a small, tight voice, as Helios bounds up and sits by him, licking at his face. Snow settles thickly over everything, including us, and there's a new, eerie silence in the aftermath of all the chaos.

'Was that Io?' I ask after a while, brushing the snow off my shoulders.

Dylan tips his head forward and shakes it from his hair.

'Is that what she does?' I ask.

'That's what she does,' he says. 'But I thought you knew all about it already.'

'I don't know everything. I know there are three sisters, Ganymede, then Io, then Callisto, my mother . . .'

'You're *related* to them all?' He looks truly horrified and it prickles at me. Even here, I'm the weird one. 'Where's your mum, then?' he demands. 'Can't you just call her to get you out of here?'

'No! I don't know . . . She left when I was small. So, no, I can't just call her.'

'You must know *something*,' he demands, though his voice is softer now.

'I know we have to get out of here,' I say, turning my back on him. 'We need to get to that little house.'

It feels like I've been stumbling around at the bottom of the hill for hours, and I'm getting nowhere. I've tried from every angle, up every curve, but my boots weren't made for mountain climbing, and the dry snow hides uneven ground. My legs are sodden up to my knees, and every time I think I've found purchase on the rocks beneath, they shift under my feet, and the whole lot tumbles down around me. My palms are bruised and scraped, my knees stiff. Every so often Dylan grumbles something behind me, and I try to ignore it, but it starts to remind me of school after a while. How can it be fair, really, to be caught up in some magical nightmare adventure with one of the people who makes my reality so flipping difficult?

'Oh, shut *up*, Dylan,' I burst eventually.

Tiny amber sparks fleck the skin of my hands as

my frustration boils over, and a web of icy veins breaks out across the ground before me. I stretch forward, frowning, and grab at a thick one. It holds as I touch it, and it feels like the roots of a tree, covered in a thin layer of snow. The fine, knobby strands thicken and spread over the hill as I watch, sending a small avalanche down to Dylan and Helios.

'What are you doing?' demands Dylan.

'Climbing to the *house*!' I shout, trying not to think too hard about what's actually happening as the roots twine further and further up the hill. My feet find purchase easily in the new tangle, my hands catch strands of twisted wood that hold firm beneath my weight.

'You're making a tree!' Dylan cries out in a strangled sort of voice, a moment later. 'There's a tree on the hill! Stop it, Clem – Io will see you!'

'It's fine!' I shout back, trying to keep calm for fear it'll all just melt away. If I lose the thread of it now, maybe the whole thing will just disappear as quickly as it appeared, and we'll be stuck at the bottom again. I keep my eyes on the ground before me, feed the sparks on my hands with sheer determination. 'I'm sure it was here already; it was probably just hibernating. Are you coming? You wanted a way out of here – this is it!'

I look back. His eyes flash like mirrors as he looks up at me, and he wraps his arms round himself, clearly not intending to budge.

'Oh for goodness' sake.' I stare at him, and then at the huge shaggy dog by his side. 'Helios!' I shout. 'Come!' He gives a little ruff, putting one paw forward. 'Come on, boy – come to me!'

'Stop that!' says Dylan, holding on to him. 'Leave him alone. He's mine!'

'Come with him, then!' I say. 'Or do you want to be stuck here forever?'

The tree is silver-grey and smooth as glass, rising up from the hill and casting shadows over all the white. I keep my eyes on it as I heave my way up the last part of the frozen ground, grabbing at the roots that curl like ribbons around me. Dylan is climbing behind me in silence, and Helios is already at the top. He scampers away and then returns to the brow of the hill, barking excitedly, his tail whipping through snow and sending it swishing down on top of us in a fine cloud.

I get to the top and take a shuddering breath, looking up at the tree, wondering how it really came to be here.

It's beautiful. Twisted, and bent to one side as if always in the same wind, its bare branches gleaming. Dylan grunts as he reaches level ground, sliding on his hands and knees away from the edge, Helios capering around him.

'How did you do that?' he asks, breathing heavily.

'I don't know,' I whisper. 'Magic?'

'Well, you are related to the monsters who made this place,' he says. 'I suppose it makes sense that *you* can make things happen too.'

'A thank you would probably do it,' I say in a tart voice, turning to the hut.

'*No*,' he whispers behind me.

'What now?'

'A storm,' he says, his eyes flicking up to the swirling dark clouds in the sky. 'Io's coming! I *knew* this would happen – you've made such a racket with all your *magic*! What's she going to say about all this? What's she going to do to us?'

'Quick, into the house,' I burst, and we scarper across the frozen ground, flinging ourselves into the wooden hut with Helios.

It's as barren and cold as it was when I first came in, and there is no flurry of magic, no sudden carpet. I'm so tired I can barely keep to my feet, so I suppose it's no wonder I can't make it happen. The storm whistles around the house and snow blows through the gaps in the wood.

'Ugh, this is miserable,' Dylan says. 'Can't believe I spent so long trying to get up here to this.'

'It was different before—' I start, but then there's a shudder and a creak – the whole room vibrates, and the walls fall away.

Dylan pushes me roughly to one side as the snow rushes in, and I trip over the wooden planks, losing my footing and tumbling back down the hill, too shocked to even scream, battered by ledge after ledge, finally landing hard on an icy patch of rock. I mean to get up, but I can't breathe. I mean to race back up there and stand by him and face Io for myself, but I can't move.

Boy! Her voice makes all the hairs on my arms stand up. It has an undercurrent of magic, a golden song that shivers through the globe and makes the whole place ring.

'Io?'

I could not see you, and now I have ruined that mean little house of yours! I shall mend it, by and by, now that you have found the courage to get there. It would be a shame if you could not use it, I suppose. But what is this, Dylan? Did you make that tree? Have you finally embraced your magic? Her voice thrills with excitement.

'I don't know how it happened. I was playing with Helios and it just appeared.'

Things do not just *appear here, boy, not without a little magic. I am glad you are finding your way to it. Perhaps now you can embrace what you have, and brighten up this place – I don't know why you have insisted upon all this snow and desolation for so long. But this tree . . . it does not feel like you, Dylan. Familiar, and yet completely unexpected!* Her mind-voice sharpens. *Have you had company?*

'No!'

There's a long silence, and the clouds darken even further; the wind sends up a great flurry of churning snow and ice.

I will take the dog away from you if you lie to me.

'I swear, I don't know what happened – please don't take him away!'

Oh, be quiet. You may have your secret, for now. I have other things to attend to. You will just have to fix your house for yourself.

There's a sharp boom, and then a tumult of blowing ice, a bitter wind that tosses the whole world around. I

74

cling to the frozen ledge and bite my lip to stop from crying out, praying she won't find me now. My hands and feet are numb with cold, and I'm half blinded by the rushing swirl of snow.

'Dylan?' I whisper, getting painfully to my knees once the storm has stopped screaming. I haul myself up, head-spinning, knees trembling, and skid down the rest of the hill to find a newly white, untrodden world. 'DYLAN!'

He doesn't answer. A loud bark is the only response, and then I see Helios kicking at the ground, where a huddled shape lies crumpled by the glass, half covered in snow.

10

Dylan doesn't stir, not even when I push him on to his back. Did Io do this? It's unnerving, how cold and still he is. Barely a lift of his chest to show he's alive.

What did Io mean about him having magic?

'Dylan? Wake up!'

If he has magic, that would make sense of his being here. But why didn't he say something? Why wouldn't he have used it already to find a way out of here? At least to get to the house.

The house!

I look up the hill. My tree spreads its snow-covered branches out to one side, and it is still beautiful, standing in isolation against the iron-grey sky. But there is no house now. Only one of the old planks is visible, and my tree is no consolation. I don't know how to get us out of here without the house.

That was the way out, and it's gone. Io didn't fix it, and I have no idea how I'd start and, even if I could, even if I rebuilt that little wooden hut, it wouldn't be the same . . . I might never find the way through to Ganymede's house.

What if we're truly stuck here now, forever?

'Dylan,' I whisper, choking back a rising tide of panic. 'Wake up!' But whatever Io did to him hasn't worn off yet. I pull at him and brush the snow and ice away from his face. 'I don't know what to do,' I whisper, looking from him to Helios, who lays his head on Dylan's chest and looks at me with huge moss-green eyes. I'm guessing he's done this before, and there's something about his loyalty that makes me feel just a little warmer on the inside. Surely, I tell myself, if Io can get in and out, so can I.

'OK,' I say to Helios. 'You stay there and keep him warm. I'll find us another way out.'

Helios huffs at me and turns his head away, and I get up, staggering to the edge of the globe where the glass rises up in a great shining dome, and put my hand against the surface. It's cold and hard, completely unyielding.

I prowl the perimeter with sharp eyes, watching for movement on the other side, pressing my fingers against it and steaming it up with my breath. There's a place where I can see the giant shapes of Ganymede's tower room, but, however hard I will it, there is no way out through there. I carry on my inspection until I'm so cold I can barely feel my nose, but there is no shift, no hole, no change at all, and when I try to make sparks fly all that happens is a dull ache deep in my belly.

Dylan is still a shape on the ground, Helios still stands over him, and I think that maybe I have made things worse. Now there isn't even the hope of getting to the house. I pound my fists against the glass with a small, repressed howl of rage. It rings with a mournful chime, and I spread my hands over it quickly, to dim the noise before Io returns.

There's a soft spot.

I run my fingers over it again, peering close. The glass here is definitely different. It warps slightly, and when I push hard it stretches, clinging to my fingers. I whip my hand away, and it bounces back into shape.

'Ew,' I whisper, prodding at it and watching as ripples

cascade away across the surface of the globe. Something shifts on the other side as I stare, and I realize I have no idea where I'll end up, if I make it through. Will it be another globe? Will a magician be waiting for me on the other side?

I back off and go to check Dylan, huddling up against Helios for a bit, tucking myself into his warmth. Dylan sleeps on and is no help at all, and Helios is pretty awesome, but even here it seems that dogs don't talk, so he's no help either. After a while I get my mother's book out and flick through the pages, but I'm not sure she was ever *inside* the globes; there's certainly no mention I can find of soft spots in the glass, or ways through magicians' prisons. I tuck the book back into my pocket with a sigh.

This bit is on me.

I get up and stomp back to the warped place in the glass, and in my haste slip on a treacherous bit of ice. My feet fly out from under me, and I land hard on my already bruised backside, cursing as I collide with the glass. I lie there for a moment, looking up at the snow-filled clouds, half wishing I were safely back at home. What will Pa be thinking? Will he even know I've gone, what with the strange way time passes in here?

'No good worrying about that *now*,' I tell myself savagely. I pull myself up on to my elbows with a sigh, and see that my foot has gone right through the glass. For a startled second, I just stare at it. My foot, in its old black boot, on the other side.

I wiggle it. It moves. When I pull it towards me, the glass around it starts to ripple. I sit up and shift myself towards the glass, and thrust my hand through, my tongue between my teeth. Then I pull my foot out and kneel on the snow, slowly putting my hand down on the other side. The ground feels hard, and scrubby. Strands that fold beneath my palm, like grass. It's warmer there, which gives me hope. Dylan could do with getting out of this cold. We all could.

'OK,' I whisper, glancing back, my heart sinking a little when I see that Dylan still hasn't woken. Helios stares at me, and I take a breath and stretch my other hand into the warm space. I take it steady, pushing myself inch by inch through the glass, breathing slowly. Both shoulders, and then my head – it's like pushing at a wall of water, just hoping I'll be able to breathe once I break through.

There's a pop, and then I can't see, can't hear anything, barely remember who I am. I'm drowning, unravelling, panicking and trapped. I try to shout, but nothing comes out, and my breath gets stuck.

Something pulls; something bites.

I yank myself back into the snowglobe, choking and spluttering. Helios bounces up at me, licking my face, his head butting against my shoulder.

'Thank you,' I breathe, putting my arms round him and resting into his warmth. I guess it was never going to be easy, but I couldn't have imagined this; it's like fighting my way into a swirl of nothingness so complete that even existing within it feels impossible.

I try again and again until despair begins to creep in. I can't do this for much longer; I'm exhausted. I brace myself and give it one last attempt, holding myself tight in my mind, aware of every movement of my limbs, every breath. I put all of my mind into it until my veins are roaring, and I push harder, reach further, until warm air is kissing my fingers, and I am in a new world.

Where a fox is staring out at me from a pile of golden leaves beneath an autumn tree.

*

When I dreamed of bravery, it was all a bit more shiny. The sun, the glint of my sword and the golden horn of a unicorn as I jumped on its back and rode down the enemy. There was a feeling of freedom about it, of leaping and whooping and punching the air. Not pushing myself through warped glass clutching a sleeping boy and really hoping the enormous dog will just follow.

'Come *on*,' I burst, tugging as the glass resists around us. I curve my back and push out behind me as hard as I can, but Dylan is heavier than I thought.

In the end, I do it with a shout of frustration and a burst of orange light, pulling and heaving until we're both all the way through.

I sit in a heap on wet grass for a while, looking at a beautiful coppery autumn tree, then prop Dylan up against the inside of the glass dome, and stick my head back into the icy world, trying desperately to ignore the strange pull of the grey stuff that swirls around my shoulders. A doggy head tilts to one side.

'Come on,' I call. 'Come!'

He whines, stretches out one paw and quickly retracts it.

'Helios, come!' I smile and wave my hands around. 'Please – he'll be cross if I leave you here. Come!'

He makes a funny little noise at the back of his throat and then leaps for me. I manage to grab a handful of bright yellow fur and brace myself on the other side, heaving until we're in a big old heap in the grass. After a moment, he shakes himself all over and bounces off into the leaves.

'You're welcome,' I whisper, looking back at Dylan. I thought he'd wake here; instead he's almost paler, as if the sun has bleached him out. Autumn leaves fly in a cool breeze, and the branches of the vast tree knock against the glass. After a few minutes, the fox bounds out of the heap of leaves at the base of its trunk.

Helios races back to me and presses himself back against the glass.

'Fox, this is Helios. Helios, this is a fox. Not going to hurt you, probably. You're too big to be food.' I shove at Dylan, and he slumps into the grass, so I heave him up, brushing leaves out of his hair. 'Sorry,' I whisper, propping him up again.

I stare at the fox and the dog, who are approaching each other, low-backed and snuffling suspiciously. 'Fox,

Helios, you'll just have to get along for a bit; we're too tired to move. As you can see.'

And I hope it isn't another spell, or Io on her way, because all of a sudden I really can't keep my eyes open. 'Keep watch, Helios,' I slur, curling up.

Dylan is still asleep when I wake, sprawled out now in the muddy grass, smiling faintly. I wonder if he knows, even through the sleep, that he's not in winter any more. That it's warmer, that the light is golden, and even the leaves are somehow comforting, in a dry, rustling sort of way. Helios stands over him, and the fox has disappeared back into its bunker beneath the leaves.

'Dylan, wake up,' I whisper. 'Please, we need to work out what to do next.'

Because actually, though it was a really good idea to get out of the snow and the cold, now we're just stuck in another world. I walk the perimeter of the globe and look out to the tower room in Ganymede's house. There's not much to make out: I can see the domed roof with its curved iron frame in the distance, and some of the shelves with the globes upon them. Mostly, though, it's just shadow. I can't even really tell what time of day it is.

Then I see the globe next to ours, where the sky is pink and tiny bright birds spiral around an ancient green sundial, a shadowed figure flitting between them in an iridescent cloak. Do we have to get in there next? How do we get out of the whole place and back to Ganymede's house? I move around the globe, testing the glass, but I can only feel that strange warp between ours and the one with the sundial; it's the only way out.

I shiver and turn my back on it, sitting by Dylan and hoping he'll wake up with some miracle idea. Helios snuffles at my hair and breathes on me, which is kind of disgusting and kind of nice all at the same time.

'Hey,' I say, putting my hands deep into his wiry coat. 'I'm glad you're here. How did you get to be here, I wonder? Are you a magician, Helios?' I grin, and he licks my face, and finally Dylan begins to stir.

'You're awake!' I say, relief flooding through me.

'Am I?'

Dylan pulls himself up and sits cross-legged, frowning. After a while, he picks up one of the copper leaves that carpet the grass. He spends a really long time looking at it, turning it over, holding it up to his nose, stroking the dry veins.

'Do you know how long it's been since I saw a leaf?' he asks, his voice still drowsy.

'A while?'

He yawns and rubs his arms. And then bounces up all in a flurry, looking from me to Helios, back at the snowy world we came from, and then at the tree.

'We're in the fox globe!'

'You noticed.'

'Is it real?'

'Yes. We've even met the fox. He's gone back to his den now.'

Dylan leans down and peers at me, frowning. His eyes are all bright and alert; the sleep has done him good. 'What's wrong?'

'It was difficult,' I say. 'And I didn't know when you would wake up, so I was a bit worried about that, and now we're here, and I don't really know what that means.'

'It means *everything*!' he flutes, throwing a handful of leaves up into the air. 'It means we can travel between globes!'

'Which is useful how?'

'If we can travel between them, we can find a way

out! You can use your magic! Thank goodness Io didn't see you; she'd have separated us for sure.'

'She said *you* have magic.' I push myself up and fold my arms, looking him in the eye, trying to see a trace of it. I've never even caught a hint that he might have magic, and yet Io sounded so sure.

He stares at me.

'Well?' I ask.

'No.'

'She sounded pretty sure to me, Dylan.'

'If I had magic, I'd have got out of here, wouldn't I? I'd have tried anything!'

'But it makes sense. My mother's book said the globes are prisons for magicians. Why would you be in here if you didn't have magic?'

'I don't know,' he breathes, closing his eyes. 'I don't want to talk about it.'

'Dylan . . .'

'What?' His eyes open and there's a flash there, something silver-blue, that I recognize immediately.

'It's OK! You don't have to hide it.'

'Oh, what do you know about it? You're not me, Clem. What else does your mother's book say about it?'

'I haven't read it all.' I sigh. 'It's a diary she wrote;

87

it's not an instruction manual or anything. And it's difficult to read . . . I only know what I've already told you. I only knew for sure that magic was real when I pushed Jago. I didn't know about any of this!'

'That was my last day out there,' he says.

'Which was yesterday, I keep telling you. Time's different here, obviously. When was the last time you had anything to eat, or drink?'

He blinks. 'Not since I've been here.'

'So you see? It's an illusion, Dylan! It's been a day, that's all. Or you'd be a skeleton by now.'

He sighs. 'So what kind of magic do you have?'

'I don't know. I'm still learning. What happened with Jago was an accident. I didn't mean to do it.'

'He was really rattled; he barely spoke for the rest of the day,' Dylan says.

'I shouldn't have done it.'

Dylan shrugs, sitting next to me. 'It's not like he didn't deserve it.'

'Why is he so fixated on me, anyway?'

'It bothers him that you're different,' he says.

I flinch. You'd think I'd be used to the idea already, but hearing it out loud makes it hurt more.

'I'm sorry. I shouldn't have said that.'

I shrug. 'It's just the truth.'

'That doesn't make it right,' he says. 'I should have made him stop. Especially if . . . if I might be different too.'

'You mean you have magic too,' I snap.

'No.' He winces. 'I don't. But I should have stopped him anyway. He's not always a total jerk. He was OK when stuff happened at home.'

'What stuff?'

'After my dad died, we moved.' He mumbles it, shuffles leaves with his feet, takes a breath. 'Mum didn't want to live by the sea any more; she knew he'd had a connection with the water, and she was worried I'd have it too. And then she met someone new. It was hard.' He takes a deep breath, stares into the sky. 'Jago was one of the first people I met when I started school. He was OK. He let me spend time at his house when I didn't want to be at mine. After that, I felt like I owed him.'

'Friendship doesn't work like that. Does it?' I stare at him. 'I didn't know about your dad. I'm sorry he died. Maybe his magic was connected to the water, and you have it too. Maybe that's what happened – you used it somehow, and Ganymede saw and locked you up.'

'I don't *know* what happened,' he says, getting up and brushing leaves off his bum. 'I'm just glad to be out of that icy place. Come on – let's see if we can get through to the next one. If we keep going, we might find Io's globe; there's bound to be a way out there.'

'I thought you were afraid of Io.' I stare at him. 'I think *I* might be afraid of Io.'

'You?' He smiles. 'I've seen what you can do. *You* don't need to be afraid of her.' He reaches down and pulls me up. 'Now, how exactly do we get through this glass?'

11

Breaking through is easier with Dylan helping. We push together at the strange warped place we find in the glass on the other side of the enormous autumn tree, and after a breathless moment emerge in the pink dawn of the next world. The air rings with birdsong, and on top of a giant sundial perches a man with pointed ears and a grey-blue cloak that opens up like wings when he jumps down on to the shining mosaic-tiled ground.

'What are you doing here?' he asks. Tiny rainbow birds flutter as he walks towards us, settling quickly on to his shoulders, their black eyes shining as they watch us. 'It is rude to burst in without invitation.'

'We're looking for a way out,' says Dylan, keeping one hand on Helios's back to stop him jumping up at the birds.

91

'Out? Out where?'

'Out of the snowglobes, to the real world,' I say.

'The real world?' The man frowns, tilting his head to one side as he inspects us, his green eyes glittering. 'Is it out, or in?'

'Is what? What?' I demand. 'What?'

'In, out – who knows,' he says. 'Does my lady know you are on the prowl?' The birds chirp softly, some of them alighting on his head. 'Yes, yes,' he says. 'My friends say you look familiar.' He stares at me. 'I do not see it, but they travel further than I do. *I* only go where I have been invited.'

'Who is your lady?'

'My lady the Great Io, of course,' he snaps, and the birds take to the air in a whir of bright, sharp wings. 'She is all powerful here, and all shall bow before her. But you do not look very magical. You just look like lost children.'

'We have a little magic,' I say.

'Do you? Then why so plain? Why do you not fly, or sparkle? Why are you so sad? I do not like it. Where is your globe? What is it like?'

'It was cold,' Dylan says.

'Why did you not warm it?'

'I . . .'

'Children –' the man shakes his head – 'you do not know what to do with yourselves. You could make anything here – my lady does not mind – so long as you are having fun! You could *be* anything – did you not see our friend the fox in there? He is a man, you know. A funny little shy man. I do not like him, but all the same I have seen him, rustling in his leaves, howling. Some of us are happy here with the worlds we have created in our globes. Some of us are having fun!'

'I was not having fun,' Dylan says, letting go of Helios, who immediately starts chasing the birds.

'No, no! Contain your hound! You must leave, miserable children!' The man flaps his wings, jumps up on to the sundial and twists it with a flourish, until the sky begins to brighten. 'Sound the alarm, my pretties,' he calls to the birds. 'We have vagabonds here. *Vagabonds!*'

Colours bleed out of the world as the ground starts to shake beneath our feet and the birds' feathers cascade around us, their sharp beaks darting like flashing knives, making the air blur. The man screeches, twisting faster and faster, his wings a silvery blur at his back, and we lower our heads, dashing around the mosaic, dragging our fingers across the glass until I find the place where it puckers.

'Here!' I shout, grabbing at Helios.

Dylan grabs my other hand, and we force our way through the glass.

We emerge underwater. Glittering starfish cling to an old wooden shipwreck, and I make for the surface, but slippery reels of golden seaweed cling to my feet. I kick at them, but they just seem to hold on tighter, wrapping round my legs. I scream, letting out a burst of bubbles, and then I'm choking, breathing in salt water.

Calm down. Dylan grabs my wrist, looks me in the eye.

I clamp my mouth shut. *Can't breathe!*

He's not panicking. He's not drowning. He's breathing underwater.

Dylan!

His eyes light up as he realizes what's happening, but there's no time for celebrating, no time for thought, even. My chest is burning, my limbs getting heavy.

What do I do? Help!

He pulls me towards him, sweeping an arm through the water. Tiny blue sparks trail from his hand. A huge bubble opens up around us, and the next breath I take isn't seawater – it's air.

'Look what you did,' I whisper, when I can find my voice again.

'I didn't know,' he says, as Helios charges into the bubble.

I reach down and untangle the trailing weeds; they're already slipping away from the air in the bubble.

'I swear – I really didn't think . . .'

'Doesn't matter now,' I say. 'Just keep doing it!'

'I never let myself even wonder,' he says, his hand still making little twisting motions. 'I kept away from the water after Dad died; I knew Mum would freak out if she ever saw that I had the same feel for it. I didn't know I could do something like this.'

He looks caught between grinning and freaking out entirely, and I don't want him to freak out right now, so I just beam at him.

'It's awesome,' I say. 'Maybe we should head for the surface, though . . .'

'But *look* at this place!' he says, gazing through the bubble. The sea is full of life. Tiny orange fish, golden starfish, long rainbow-coloured eels that wind like ribbons through the deep blue. Coral unfurls all around us in shades of pink and purple, and the wreck is covered in clusters of moon-bright barnacles. 'Let's explore,' he says. 'It's an old pirate ship – look at the flag – there must be treasure on here. I'm sure I saw gold . . .'

'We're not on a treasure hunt!' I say, but his new enthusiasm is infectious, and a moment later I dart after him towards the dark hulk of the ship, the bubble dragging with us.

The deck is slippery with algae, and the mast creaks ominously when I brush up against it. I take courage from the sight of the sun through the clear water; I've never been much of a swimmer. Helios chases the tiny little azure fish that venture into our bubble, and Dylan is like a seal, swishing this way and that, lifting wood panels and diving down to explore the deep.

Eventually he hauls a chest up on to the deck with a look of triumph on his face. He pokes and pries it, and I join him. The padlock is old and rusted, and when we heave against it together it breaks, and the lid of the trunk swings open, revealing piles of gold coins and glittering stones.

'Wow,' breathes Dylan as the sea around us darkens, the pull of the tide getting stronger. 'Look at this!' He puts his hand in and grabs a handful of gold, flourishing it at me and sprinkling most of the coins over the deck. 'Gold, Clementine – real gold!'

I giggle. He sounds like a pirate. But when I go to take in a breath again, I choke on a mouthful of salty water – the bubble has burst. Dylan stares at me in a panic and grabs hold of my hand, kicking towards the surface as the sea turns black, a sudden storm making violent riptides that swirl and tear us apart. I'm lost in an inky nightmare – I can't see anything, can't tell which way is up or down. Strange pale shapes flutter about me, coiling around my ankles until I can't kick any more, and when I scream, there's no sound, just a rush of bubbles. My chest is bursting, the sea is an endless weight, and darkness creeps in the corners of my eyes, as I'm turned head over heels.

A slim hand reaches out and takes me by the arm, pulling me hard. There's a flash of silvery scales, a giant fish tail, barely visible through the murk, and Dylan's pale face, staring into mine as we're pulled to the surface, Helios at our heels.

We emerge into the full force of the storm. Lightning strikes, and the waves are screaming giants that swoop down and would crush us but for the figure that holds us tight, darting through the water and emerging, again and again, until the worst is over, and the sea is just a cold, choppy mass of black beneath a cloud-filled sky.

Her skin is moon-bright, her hair as inky as the sea, piled up on her head and winking with tiny golden starfish. When she finally lets go of us, it's colder than ever, and my teeth chatter so hard I can't speak.

'Mer . . .' manages Dylan, his eyes wide as lamps. '. . . maid.'

'So you have heard of me,' she hisses through needle-sharp teeth.

'What happened?' I stammer.

'Storm.' She shrugs. 'Your boy's magic isn't a match for that. You were unlucky. Or lucky that I was close by. Either way, you will be safe now. The sun will break through, by and by. Do not linger here, though; this is *my* sea, and Io is on the prowl. She will not like me helping you.'

I stare at her, shivering and small, treading water with bone-weary legs.

'Are you a magician?'

'I am a mermaid!'

'You made yourself like this?' Dylan frowns. 'Was it

like this when you were locked up in here, or did you make the sea?'

'It was snow,' she says with a shudder. 'And I was angry for a while; I had not done much to deserve being locked away. One little storm I made, to teach a boy a lesson, and here I was. There was no way out.' She flips her tail and stares at the rainbow-coloured scales. 'But I always liked the sea, and my lady Io said I could make my world as I wished, so I made it thus.' She looks around with pride at the rolling waves, the white horses that break on the surface, and then her eyes flick up to the storm clouds, still lingering. 'I never really cared for children, though, and my lady does not either.' She gives us a toothy grin. 'She has smelt you, little ones; she is on your trail!' And she turns and dives down into the sea just as the clouds part.

'Quick,' says Dylan. 'We need to get out of here before she finds us.'

It's not so easy to find a shimmery bit of glass in a world of water. We swim out until we find the edge, both of us constantly on the lookout for any sign of Io, but there's no thin place at the surface. Eventually, as blue skies open up around us, we have to dart down. I search the glass while Dylan keeps a new bubble around us with his strange, fluttering motions. His eyes spark, but the air is thin, and beneath all the magic, he looks exhausted. By the time I find the whorl in the glass, he's drooping, and I have to catch hold of his shirt to drag him through, Helios lumbering after.

12

It's cold in the next world. Wind whips at our wet clothes, and a light drizzle begins to fall. Ahead of us up a flight of pale wooden steps is a square yellow building with a wide door, bright light spilling out.

'Come on –' I pull at Dylan – 'it'll be warmer.'

'Wait a sec,' he says, stumbling and sitting heavily on the bottom step. 'I just need to catch my breath.' He draws Helios in close between us and rests his forehead against the back of his neck.

I pull out my mother's book, sodden now with water, and peel a few of the pages apart. The writing is completely smudged, the sketch at the front barely recognizable. I take a deep breath and blow gently, hoping that somehow when it's dry it will be restored. The pages crinkle, the leather is stained and only the odd word is now legible. I tuck it under my arm, tears stinging at my eyes, but I tell myself it doesn't matter – maybe it will somehow recover itself in this magical place.

Dylan doesn't stir, and after a while my skin starts to itch from all the drying saltwater. We can't stay here forever.

'Dylan? Are you all right?'

He looks up at me. 'I don't know.'

'Because of the magic?'

He nods. 'It feels like I left a little bit of me in there, when I did that. It was like I was pouring myself out, and now there's a hole.'

'You're tired,' I say. 'You put a bit of yourself into it – you had to, or we'd have both drowned. It'll come back, though. You'll feel better in a bit.'

'Is this how it feels when you do it?'

'I haven't really done very much,' I say. 'I mean, I got into your globe, and then I got us through to the fox – I suppose that must have been magic. And that day with Jago. But those are all just moments, little flashes of time. You used yours for quite a while in there; it's bound to have an effect. Especially because it was the first time.'

'*Nearly* the first time,' he says, closing his eyes.

'What do you mean?'

'I think . . . maybe . . . I did something the day I ended up in my globe. I didn't mean to, but I was walking home and thinking about you and Jago, that flicker in your eye. I'd seen it in my dad before, and I wondered if maybe I could do it too. When it started to rain, I flicked a few drops away.' He motions with his thumb and forefinger. 'But that was all; it was nothing. And then everything turned upside down, and I was in a snowstorm, and I didn't know where I was, or what was going on. For a while, I was so busy trying to get up the hill, trying to break through the glass, I didn't even remember I'd done it, and then when I did I told myself I was just being silly, after all that time on my own in the globe. I never wanted magic; it scared me. Even when Io told me I should use it . . . I didn't even let myself try.'

'It doesn't matter now,' I say, frowning at the slur in his voice. He sounds as if he's already asleep, and we can't rest here. We have to keep going, find our way out before all of our energy is used up on fleeing from these strange worlds.

'My dad had magic, and it didn't save him,' he says,

opening his eyes and squinting at me. 'Why didn't he use it to save himself?'

'Maybe he tried?' I take a deep breath; it's hard to find the right words. 'I don't know. But it can't be all bad, Dylan. I mean, you just saved our lives!'

'Yeah.' He smiles, and lets me haul him up. 'I'm a regular hero.'

But he stumbles up the steps after me, and as much as I'm aching and cold, and more tired than I've ever been before, he's clearly feeling even worse. We have to get out of here while he's still moving.

My heart leaps when we traipse into the dry warmth of a library. The front desk is an ornate pulpit, and shelves run from floor to ceiling for as far as the eye can see, all of them full of books that seem to have been ordered according to their size and colour. Somewhere here, there must be a clue. One of these books must have something that will tell us how to get out of here.

'All this water, in my *library*!' shrieks a voice as a man wearing a velvet coat rushes towards us, flapping his hands, his top hat wedged firmly on to his curly silver hair. 'How dare you! Get out – get off my parquet floor! Stop dripping! And what's this – a dog? In the library? A boy, and a *girl* . . . half drowned . . . and a dog . . .' He slows, his tone changing, recognition dawning. 'How *curious.*'

'Why curious?' I ask.

'There aren't many who travel through our worlds,' the man says. 'And you alone are untethered – I can see it!' He stares at me. 'Did you enter this place under your own *volition?*'

'I came in . . . I came to get my friend out,' I say, backing up as Helios shakes himself, fat droplets scattering among the bookshelves.

'*Interesting.*' He scowls at Helios. 'But no matter, no matter,' he says after a deep breath, his eyes sparkling. 'I have you now. All those whispers of strange children, and here you are! I shall keep you –' his eyes flick to the open door of the library – 'I shall keep you safe. You look in need of answers, my dears. May I help?'

'Who are you?'

'My name is Timothy,' he says. 'I am the librarian, clearly. Oh, and I see you have a book! Let me see, my dear. Let me see!'

'Uh, no, you're all right,' I manage. 'It's just a diary, and it got a bit wet, so it's probably useless now.'

'Not with the correct preservation,' he says, pushing the front of his hat back to mop at his brow with a white hankie. 'This is not a common lending library, you know. This is a *magical* library, and I am very good with books. I have to be – in here are books of such power, they could turn your kidneys into roses, or curse the whole world to eat nothing but spaghetti for a year! Now, let me see . . .'

He flicks his fingers, and the book, tightly wedged under my arm, flies out towards him.

'Stop!' I gasp, and the book flutters in mid-air, caught between us.

Timothy's eyebrows shoot up with surprise that turns to outrage when the book flies back my way.

'Ooh, what a child.' He pouts. 'Truly you do belong in here, don't you? All that magic just wriggling around inside, waiting to pounce. And did I see the *Paradis* name there? I think I did!'

'We should get out of here,' Dylan whispers, backing towards the door.

But I can't move. I can't just turn away, not when Timothy's eyes gleam like that. Not when he knows something about my mother's book. Not when he's in charge of a whole library that might tell me all the things we need to know. How to get out.

Where my mother is.

'Tell me how I can help you, my dears,' Timothy says. 'No judgement here: whatever your problems, whatever you need, I'm sure we can find a way!'

His eyes glitter. I don't trust him. He's probably on Io's side, just waiting for the chance to call out to her. Maybe if we can divert him, I can search for the book that will tell us how to get home. There must be one somewhere. We just need to distract him and find it before he alerts Io.

'We're looking for unicorns,' I say, ignoring Dylan's wild-eyed stare and looking Timothy square in the eye. 'Perhaps if you had a book on one . . . ?'

He nods. 'Unicorns are indeed both magical and popular. Let me help you. Let me see . . .'

He climbs on to the first rung of the ladder and starts to scoot it along, getting faster and faster, smaller and smaller. And then he whizzes back. '*Stay right there,*' he barks at us. '*No browsing!*'

I nod, and we watch him scoot off again.

'OK,' I say, turning to Dylan.

He's gone a bit pale.

'What's wrong?'

'I'm fine,' he says with a wan smile. 'What are you doing asking about unicorns?'

'Just distracting him. You sit with Helios for a bit, and I'll see if I can find something about getting out in one of these books . . .' I say, and he nods, slumping down on to the wooden floor with one arm round Helios.

I start off down the shelves, kicking up golden-yellow dust as I go, watching it spool off the shelves closest to me. *Please*, I say, deep in my mind where I hope my magic is listening. *Show me what I need.* I think it, over and over, imagining the globes, the house where Ganymede stalks, keeping it all live in my mind, and reaching out at random, traipsing through the aisles, just hoping Timothy has gone far enough that he's not about to pop out at me. He seemed to recognize us just from our appearance, and goodness knows what he'll make of the Paradis name. I guess it's my mother's maiden name, and so it would be Io and Ganymede's name too. I wonder how many worlds we'll have to go through before we find our way out. What we'll see along the way.

My mother?

The thought flashes, bright as a star, and my chest hitches.

No. I promised I'd get Dylan out of here, and that's what I'm going to do. My mother, wherever she is, is a powerful woman. Pa told me so, many times. If she were here, she could get out by herself. If she were here, she could find me.

'Snowglobes,' I mutter to myself, running my fingers along the shelves.

A book about snowdrops pushes itself out. I pick it up, flick through and tut at myself. 'Snow*globes*,' I say. '*The magic of snowglobes, and how to get out!*' I wedge the book back on to the shelf and make for the next aisle.

'What are you doing?' thunders the man in the top hat, popping up when I get to the end. 'You are *browsing*!'

'It was difficult to stay still,' I say, clamping my mother's diary even tighter under my arm. 'You have so many beautiful books.'

'I do, 'tis true,' says the man. 'Always loved books, you know. Read my first when I was two and been reading ever since. These are no ordinary books, though, girl! You may not flounce willy-nilly through these shelves!'

'No, I see. I'm sorry. Did you find anything?'

'Plenty, plenty.' He sighs. 'Not the one you're looking for, though. You want to know about unicorns, no?' His eyes narrow suspiciously.

'Yes, unicorns.'

'I'll look again,' he says. 'And I suppose you may wander my shelves, if you like. But don't touch – some of them bite!' He grins, revealing yellowed, papery teeth, and scurries off again.

After a moment, he swings past me on his ladder, about halfway up this time, propelling himself with great sweeps of his arm.

'Anon!' he calls.

I dart down the next aisle, and the next, and the next, until finally I stumble upon a glass case, a small book resting on a cushion inside, a sketch of a snowglobe on the outside. '*Instruction and Destruction*,' says the title, '*and Everything in Between*'.

I frown at the way the *ins* seem to glow. It seems familiar, as though it's trying to tell me something I've already heard.

'Ooh, you've found my treasure,' says the man, scuttling back over to me. 'That one is a biter, for sure!'

'Really?'

He scowls. 'Yes. And I have just remembered that

my book about unicorns is already out on loan.'

'Oh, I'm sorry about that.'

He stares at me. 'My lady is a little partial to a unicorn herself.' He taps his foot against the wooden floor.

'What do you mean?' I ask, my mouth dry. 'Do you mean Io? Is she your lady? Have you already told her we're here?' My voice rises, and I back away from him. I'd thought I was diverting him, but perhaps he's already found a way to alert her.

'No, no, not at all; I'm trying to help you!' he says, but his eyes are shifty, his forehead more shiny than ever as he hurries after me.

I turn and rush back towards Dylan.

'You must stay here. I insist. I cannot let you continue to roam, with all your magic and your little secret book that shouts of magical royalty! I have questions! I need to have that book – you must wait!'

'Get up!' I shout, running back the way I came. 'Dylan! We have to get out!'

'No, my dear!' Timothy laughs, sweeping after me on his ladder. 'Where do you think you're going? You think that getting out of here will be so simple? My lady is coming; she wants to *meet* you!'

'We have to go,' I mutter, as Dylan struggles to his feet. 'Io's on the way – we have to go *now!*

'What are you doing?' Timothy demands as we head for the door.

'We're going to get some air,' I say. 'That's all.'

'Oh no . . .' He shakes his head. 'Oh no, that's not the plan.'

The wooden doors shut with a bang, the lights dim and the yellow dust begins to spiral around us. The man's eyes light up.

'Oh, she is coming,' he murmurs, clasping his hands together. 'Wait here, children! I must find my good hat . . .' He strides to the ladder and propels it into motion, stepping on to the bottom rung.

I look at Dylan, and he looks at me. His eyes are ringed with fatigue, his fingers trail over Helios's coat, as if he's all that's keeping him upright.

'What do we do now?' he asks. 'She's going to find us, Clem, and she won't let us out! All this time, she never let me out, and you're her family – he said it was on that book of yours – she's not going to just let you go!'

'We just need to stay ahead of her until we have a plan,' I say. 'We'll find a way, Dylan. Starting with getting out of here!'

I stride to the door, put my fingers on the big brass lock and push at it with my mind, my blood singing, my whole self tuned in and questing for freedom. *OPEN!* I command, and the library rings with my unspoken voice as the doors blow outward, landing in a heap of splintered wood at the bottom of the steps. There's a scream behind us and a rush of whizzing wheels across the polished floor, but we don't linger.

We tumble out, our fists battering against the glass at the edge of the globe, running, running. Timothy is behind us, and a storm is brewing in the yellow clouds over our heads, but finally Dylan's hand goes through the globe. In the world before us, we can see nothing but a riot of colour and activity, a blaze of red and gold, a rush of fire, and the roar of a tiger.

We plunge headlong into it.

13

The whole world is a roar of sound and light. Stars wink in a velvet-blue sky and, before us, a circus tent has been pitched in a vast field. The grass is high, and the stalks of poppies dance with cornflowers as performers stride in and out of the tent, their costumes dazzling, music blaring. Little stalls have been set up under striped awnings, and the sellers shout while acrobats whirl past, juggling fiery torches, throwing spangled hoops high into the air.

We stand in the shadows watching unseen, until the tiger saunters past us. Helios whimpers and hides behind our legs, but the tiger doesn't stop. It just stares at us with unblinking amber eyes, before loping off into silver woodland at the edge of the field.

'That was weird,' Dylan says.

'Everything is weird,' I reply tiredly. 'The tiger's the least of it. Did you *want* it to eat us?'

'No. But the way it stared and then ran off . . .'

'Oh.' I look after it towards the tall, bare winter trees.

'Like maybe it's a spy for Io?' Dylan says. 'Gone to get her.'

'Let her come,' I say. 'I'm tired of running. I'll tell her who I am, and ask her how to get out of here.'

Dylan shakes his head. 'You have no idea what you're talking about. You think she'll care who you are? You won't get straight answers out of Io, whoever you are. You'll be lucky if you can find your voice at all.'

'So what do you suggest?'

'Someone here might help us,' he says, looking around. 'They can't all be on her side, enjoying their prisons.'

'Timothy seemed to be. It's all an illusion anyway, Dylan. When I was in the house in your globe, it started to become home . . . the same rug, pictures on the wall. Whatever you imagine, I suppose. Why did you imagine *snow*?'

'I don't remember imagining it,' he says. 'It was just there. I'd have changed it if I could . . .' He hesitates, looking at me. 'I could have, couldn't I?'

'Maybe.' I shrug. 'If you'd really believed in your magic. You weren't ready.'

'Do you think these are all magicians, then?' he says. 'Coming together for a *circus*?'

'Let's ask someone and find out.'

We venture in closer, watching the acrobats warm up as clowns stalk through on stilts, and we steal candyfloss from a stall while the vendor juggles cups, and though it tastes of nothing it makes Dylan's eyes shine.

'Dad used to take me to the circus,' he says as we start towards the main tent.

Whispers follow, and the bright eyes of the performers are on us, but he doesn't seem to notice, and I don't think I trust them enough to ask for help. I pull us into the shadows.

'It came every summer, and we'd have candyfloss, and he'd get me one of those light-up whizzy wands, and we'd sit and watch together. He loved it, loved seeing magic happen. He always said one day he'd show me real magic, but he died before he could . . .' He holds up the candyfloss and it sparkles in the torchlight. 'It's just an illusion, though, isn't it? The food, the lights – none of it's real.'

'It was real when you went with your dad,' I say, noticing the stalls are getting quieter now, the performers heading towards the main tent. 'I'm sorry he died before he could show you more.'

'Mum blamed the magic,' Dylan says. 'She said it drew him to the sea, even when he should have known better. There was a storm one night, and he'd taken our little boat out . . .' He stares up at the star-filled sky, his voice dropping to a murmur. 'They found him, a couple of days later. So I guess magic can't do everything. It didn't save him.'

'No,' I say, watching as a lone figure comes towards us, a woman dressed all in black. 'It saved us, though, Dylan. *You* saved us, when we were trapped under the sea.'

'Yeah, I guess so.'

The woman steps in front of us. Her black dress is threaded through with silver, her veil drawn back from her lined face, sweeping over her head and down her back. 'Do you have the *in*structions?' she whispers. 'Poor dears, you have been looking all the time for the way to get *out*. We've been trying to tell you, we who can – you must get back *in*.'

'In?'

117

'*In*, to Ganymede's house and back to your own reality,' she hisses. 'You, my girl, who wandered in of her own magic, who *wanted* to be here, you alone are not under Io's control! All these other souls are under her spell, building illusions in the sky, happy with fresh air and their dreams.' She tuts. 'Not many of us remember what this is, my dear. It is a *prison*, and I know it. And so do *you*. So it must be you. Find your way back into the house and back to reality, and then you will be free!' Her brown eyes shine. 'You are strong, my dear. Perhaps if you are free, there will be hope for all of us . . . You smell of the earth and the flowers. You look just like the one who—'

We are quickly surrounded by a huge mob of magicians all wanting to get inside the tent, and she melts into the crowd. Dylan grabs my hand and we're shoved along into the tent, just as the music starts up again.

The one who what?

Who do I look just like?

A whirling, sparkling show has unfurled on the stage ahead of me. There are trapeze artists tumbling through the air, torches burning, clowns juggling and all I can see is that old woman's eyes. All I can hear is her voice.

You look just like the one who . . .

I realize I have been wondering, as we travelled through these worlds, whether she might be here somewhere. I've tried to block it out, to focus on just getting me and Dylan out of here alive. But it's been building, and now I can't stop imagining. She didn't mean Io, because she would have said 'my lady'. So there must be someone else here who I look like.

My mother? Is she here?

The faces of the magicians are glowing against the lick of flames upon the stage. There are men and women of all ages, each of them with their own bright spark of magic. All of them – magicians, prisoners – nodding and happy under Io's spell. I search the crowds until my head spins, looking for something familiar, hoping for just a glimpse of something I haven't seen for nearly ten years. Would I recognize her, even if she was here?

Dylan nudges me. Helios lies across our feet, his eyes closed, turned away from the tumult on stage, but Dylan is entranced . . . and now the lights dim, now the music fades.

We turn and stare with the rest of the crowd as Io

enters, and all the starry lights in the fabric ceiling glow. The torches around the edges of the tent wink to golden life, so that she's in the middle of a storm of light, the tiger by her side. Her cloak is a rustling tapestry of copper and green, the hood lined with fur, and golden butterflies shiver in her long, wheat-coloured hair. Io doesn't walk – she seems almost to glide – and as she sweeps up on to the stage, there's a collective intake of breath.

'There will be no show today,' she says softly, sitting on the edge of the stage, the tiger settling by her side. 'For there are traitors in our midst. Traitors, and interlopers.' She smiles, fondles the tiger between his ears. 'Some of you have tried to waylay them, so that I might meet them for myself. Some of you have tried to *help* them to get away.' Her eyes glitter, but the smile remains. 'It does not matter, either way. I am your lady, and this is our world. All who are here are under my protection. Have you not had fun? Have I not looked after your every whim? Did I not, *Dylan*, bring you that divine puppy, that you might have warmth, when you denied your own magic and locked your*self* in the bitterest winter?'

Her eyes meet his, and he stiffens by my side. The

other magicians slowly filter away until it's just the two of us, standing before her. The music stops. The performers are gone.

'It was a sad, lonely place in which you found yourself,' she says, sliding down from the stage and coming towards us, the butterflies open-winged, nestled in her hair. 'I thought I did you a kindness, Dylan, when I stopped by. When I brought you company. I gave you a puppy! I gave you a house, but you never even tried to get there, so defiant you were. So determined to refuse your magic. And now this girl, this one small creature, comes in and changes everything! I have felt your power, Dylan! I have felt your travels. I have watched you walk through walls – do you think I was not leading you here all along?' Her eyes spark, and the tent sways around us, its walls silently crumpling to the ground until we are standing before her in a cold, starlit field. 'Do you not realize I can do *anything* here? This is my realm!'

'But you have no control over me,' I say, clutching the fortune teller's words tight against this woman, my aunt, holding her at bay even as the golden sense of her floods through the field, and the sky fades to a pale, new dawn.

'Who *are* you?' she demands, stooping to look more

closely, a movement that makes me think of Ganymede.

Around us, the flowers turn to stalks of barley and wheat, and the air gets warmer. Dylan stares at Io, his cheeks flushed. He wavers on his feet, and there is nothing for him to hold on to except me. I realize with a sharp pang of fear that we truly are alone. Helios isn't here.

'Where's Helios?' I demand.

'Oh, he is with my friends.' She smiles. 'I decided you did not deserve him. He is safe.' She waves a hand at my alarm. 'And Dylan may have him back, once he has recovered his senses. I do not harm any here, little girl, not any who are loyal to *me*. Who are *you*?'

'My name is Clementine,' I say, putting power behind the words so they sparkle in the air. Poppies and cornflowers begin to bloom between the dry grass once more, and Io startles as she watches them take over the field.

'I am Clementine. I am Callisto's daughter!'

A sudden rage swells through me, because this is my aunt, and she should *know* who I am. Green leaves break out on the silver trees in the distance, and birds start to sing; the flowers open their mouths, and their scent is powerful. Io stares at me, and I stare back,

122

drawing myself up so I'm nearly as tall as she is. Nearly as fierce.

'Callisto?' She turns as if searching for something. Some*one*. 'What is this?' she demands of me. 'Callisto has no *daughter* – I would know!'

Butterflies cascade from her, swirling in the air like bright copper pennies, and her fists clench by her sides. The sky ripens to a vibrant blue, my magic fades and petals begin to rain down on us.

'How did you get in here? I do not know what magic this is, but I will not have it here! Ganymede did not put you here; you are not bound. How did you get *IN*?'

In! In! Like a bell chiming, it rings, and that is it, I realize. The magicians have been giving us hints all along, and it was on the book in the library too; the word we need is *in*. The trick is to get back *in*to Ganymede's house. It isn't *out* at all. This is not a world, not a real place – this is a snowglobe. The house is reality, and we need to get back *in*to it.

I grab Dylan's hand and pull him away while Io raises her hands to the sky and begins to screech, turning in a whirl of gold. The ground shakes beneath us, great chasms opening as we flee to the glass boundary. Io starts after us, her words catching, making Dylan flinch, but I don't let go of him. I just keep running until I see the darkness on the other side, the darkness of Ganymede's house.

'Let us *IN*!' I scream, pounding one desperate hand upon the glass, as my feet start to flounder on a tide of ripped-up earth.

There's a ringing sound, a pull on my heart and we are through.

We are back in the house.

14

Our feet, our knees, our hands. A hard, pale marble floor that ends the journey with a sharp smack, a breathless whirl of snowglobes all shaken up, and my magic curling away, exhausted, broken. We push ourselves to stand with our backs against a wall, and Ganymede flies down the staircase towards us, skirts rustling, moths scattering as light bulbs ping, and the globes begin to flicker.

'What *happened?*' she demands.

'We got out of there,' I whisper.

Everything hurts; I can barely breathe through the tightness in my chest. I gather myself together, reach out for Dylan and we stagger to the front door, turning our backs on her.

'What are you doing? Where do you think you're

going?' She rushes with a bustle of feathered grey skirts to stand before us.

'Home!' I shout.

The globes dim, and Ganymede's hair is like wire standing on end in the gloom.

'You're not leaving until you explain yourself,' she says, swishing closer.

'*I* have explaining to do?' I demand, too tired and heartsore to be afraid of her. '*You're* the one with all the secrets, locked away here in your old tomb! You're the one who should be explaining. But it's late, and we're tired from fighting our way through all the stupid worlds you made, and we're going *home*!'

We edge past her, leaving her speechless in a whirl of storming snowglobes, and I reach out with a shaking hand to open the vast front door. We totter down the steps past all the reaching thorns and brambles, and if I turn round, I know I'll see the silhouette of my aunt, standing all alone in that ivory tower. But we don't turn round, and she doesn't stop us, so we just keep going down the path and through the gate until we're back in our town where the streetlights glow golden, and the cars swish past in a blur of headlights.

'We made it,' I say, my voice a torn whisper.

'No,' says Dylan, his voice slurring. 'Helios. We have to go back for Helios.'

He strains against me, fighting to get back into that nightmare house so that we can find his dog, who came through so much and never complained, but we can't. Tears spring to my eyes – I'd brought us back even though it meant leaving him there. I didn't even think; there was no time. And there is no more magic left in us now. No more energy. There is barely enough to keep us on our feet.

'He'll be OK,' I whisper.

Dylan just stares at me.

'We'll go back, Dylan, I promise.'

'We shouldn't have just left him there,' he says in a broken, hollow voice.

'We had no choice,' I say, trying to keep my own voice level. 'Io took him. She said he'd be safe . . .'

'And you *trusted* her?'

'There was no time; she would have trapped us all if we'd stayed! And I don't think we can make it back there like this, past Ganymede, into Io's chaos. We might never find him. We have to sleep, and eat, and then we can go back for him.' It sounds so weak, pleading. My skin tightens as I say it – how can we even think of food and warm beds, of home, when our friend has been left behind?

'He was all I had in there.'

'I'm so sorry,' I whisper. 'He'll be OK. I'm sure he will – just until we go back.'

Dylan seems to fold, and I remember the way Helios was always there, keeping him up on his feet, keeping him going, keeping us *both* going.

'Tomorrow?' He looks at me.

I swallow hard.

'Tomorrow,' I say, putting my hand on the small of his back and propelling him homeward. 'I promise.'

'Is this really our town?' he asks blearily as we start walking.

It's night, and the streetlamps are spotlights that take us in from the darkness, just for an instant, before spitting us out again. I'm telling myself that it's good to be back, but right now this place feels just as harsh as any of the worlds we fought our way through.

'Clem? Is this really home?'

'I think so,' I say as a car swooshes past us, throwing up water from a vast puddle. 'It doesn't feel like a snowglobe. I'm not sure Io can do traffic . . .'

'I s'pose not,' he says as we edge around the old common. He bumbles along, sometimes nudging into me, sometimes into the railings by the side of the pavement, like ping-pong with a broken human instead of a ball.

'Which way now?' I ask, when we come out on to the main road. 'Up here? What road is it, Dylan?'

'You can just leave me here,' he says.

'No,' I say. 'I want to make sure you get there.'

'How long do you think I've been gone in real time?' He looks up at the sky, as if the answer might be there, in the shifting clouds.

'I don't know,' I say. 'It can't be as long as we think; not if you thought you were there for months and it was only a day.' I'm hoping Pa won't have been worried out of his mind for a week. I made him a promise, and I broke it. I'm just hoping he never needs to know. 'Come on – which way?'

Dylan grunts, gesturing to the right, and we start off, a little unsteadily, making our way through winding narrow streets until finally he stops at a little terraced house. It's tucked in tight between its neighbours, the curtains drawn against the night.

'Here?'

'Yep. You can go now.' He smiles at me, but I know that smile: it's lying.

'What's wrong?'

'Nothing,' he says. He squares his shoulders and heads through the gate, finds his keys in his pocket and drops them, stoops to pick them up and wobbles, looking back at me.

'What is it?'

'I'm just tired.' He gives me a wan smile.

'And you haven't eaten real food for a long time . . .'

'Yeah.'

'It's going to be OK,' I say. 'We got out of there, Dylan. We got away from Io . . . They'll be happy to see you, won't they?'

'Probably.' He stares at the keys. 'But we left Helios there. And everything feels different now, and *they* won't know any of it. They'll expect me to be just the same, and I'm not! What about Helios, Clem? What are we going to *do*?' His eyes are full of tears.

'Nothing more today,' I say firmly as his knees buckle. I shove my hand under his elbow and pull him to the front door, knocking hard against the wall while he messes with the keys.

The door flings open and a woman rushes out, throwing her arms around him.

'Dylan! Where have you been? We were so worried!'

'Were you?' he mumbles, raising his head and looking past her at the man standing in the hallway with a baby against his shoulder.

'Of course we were! Where were you?' She pulls back and looks between us, still worried. 'What happened? Come in, both of you. You look half frozen.'

The woman drags him in, and I follow, too dazed to argue with her. It's bright in here, and warm. It smells of dinner, and normal things that make my eyes sting. I can't believe we're really here. Io's fiery eyes still flash at me every time I close mine; the ground still rolls beneath my feet.

My mother was there. I know it. And I left.

'I went to Jago's,' Dylan says as the woman hustles us into a sitting room at the front of the house, where a real fire flickers, and lamps make pools of light that shine on bookshelves and an old piano crammed in under the stairs. 'I meant to call you, but I couldn't find my phone, and I fell asleep . . . This is Clem.'

'I found him on his way home,' I say. 'I wanted to make sure he got here in one piece. I think he's got the flu or something; he hasn't been making much sense . . .'

'I'll make some tea,' the man says, dawdling in the doorway with the baby. 'Come on, Bea – let's find something to cheer up your brother.'

Dylan scowls in his direction, flopping on to a settee heaped with bright cushions.

'Oh don't.' His mum frowns, sitting next to him. 'Honestly, you're a mess, Dyl. What happened to you? Why didn't Jago's parents call me?'

'They're away,' he says, closing his eyes and leaning his head back against the wall behind the settee.

I perch on the edge of a small green armchair, watching how she looks at him, touches his hand, his brow, checking, checking all the time that he's OK.

He waves her away. 'I'm fine.'

She huffs and turns to me. 'Thanks for seeing him home, Clem. Are your parents expecting you back? I'll drive you.'

I smile. I can't speak right now.

She pats my hand and gets up, saying something about Bea's bedtime. I look around at all the stuff in the room. There's a basket of toys in one corner, a little pile of blankets and cushions on the pale carpet.

Pictures line the shelves: a knock-kneed Dylan on the beach with a man who has the same kind brown eyes beneath a thatch of brown-grey hair; a newborn Bea; and a wedding photo of Dylan's mum and the man in the hallway.

'He's your stepdad?'

'Yep.'

'He seems OK . . .'

'He is OK.'

'Bea's sweet.'

'Yep.'

I push myself up. I don't belong here. 'I should go.'

'Better let Mum take you; she'll worry.'

What does that feel like? I wonder.

Dylan looks at me. 'You think she was in there? Your mum, I mean?'

'I think she is,' I whisper. *And we left.*

'We'll go back,' he says, and he sounds far more sure about it than I am, because I can't help wondering why she's been in there for so long. Why she's never fought her way home to me.

If I managed it, why couldn't she?

15

Dylan's mum's car is a mess of kids' toys and old wrappers, and the footwells are muddy. She catches me noticing.

'Football,' she says. 'Gets boggy, watching in the winter. Where to, then?'

I give her the road name, and she winds the car through streets that get more and more narrow.

'*Oosh.*' She winces, rounding her shoulders as she manoeuvres past all the parked cars. 'You're right in the heart of it here, aren't you! Which one is yours?'

I point up at the redbrick terrace, the wrought-iron balcony that marks our flat.

'Pretty!' she says. 'I always liked these old houses. Go on, your parents will be waiting.'

'My pa,' I say.

'Your pa,' she repeats.

There's a little silence. I concentrate on the whirr of the engine and the warm air flooding through the vents.

'I'll watch you in. Thank you for getting Dyl back. He wanders. Perhaps you have that in common?'

She stares at me, and I wonder if it shows: that magic that she ran away from, the magic that lost her a husband – that grows even now in her son.

'A bit, maybe,' I say. 'Thanks for the lift.'

She nods, and watches me all the way to the red front door, waving once I'm inside. I wave back and close the door slowly, leaning against it for a moment before heading up to our flat. Every step is harder than the last; every movement drags with tiredness. I run a hand over the internal door when I finally get there, feeling the places where the blue paint dripped, remembering the day we did it, the mess we got into.

I take a breath, shove my key into the lock and tip myself into the flat, my eyes smarting at the sudden heat and all the sense of it: the wood polish from my little cleaning spree earlier; the framed prints on the ochre walls. The leafy plant that sits on the little table bursts into tiny pink flowers as my eyes fall on it, and I step closer, but then Pa comes out of his study.

His glasses are wedged into his firebrush hair, his feet scuff over the old floorboards and his eyes have that tired, worried look that means I'm in trouble. I swallow hard, and something breaks, deep inside me. The thing that kept me going, and never let me stop. The thing that buried how scared I was – that I'd never see him again, never be here again.

'Pa!' I choke, rushing at him.

He staggers back, puts his arms around me and when he asks me what's wrong his voice rumbles in his chest and it feels like home. We really made it, Dylan and I; we really made it home.

'Clem? What happened?'

'Quite a lot,' I whisper into his shirt, after a while.

He draws me away from him, peering at me, his brow furrowed.

'Tell me. Come into the study and tell me.'

The *study* is a bit of a posh term for the room where Pa works, translating ancient texts. It's the smallest room in the flat, and his desk is an old kitchen table tucked under the eaves. There's a settee slumped against the opposite wall, an old wooden filing cabinet in one corner and a globe on a stand in front of the tiny window.

Pa sits on his desk chair and points the Anglepoise lamp at me.

'No.' I wince, flumping into the settee. 'Too bright.'

He swings it up at the ceiling. 'Where were you?'

'I did leave you a note . . .'

'You said you were at Lizzie's house. But I phoned to make sure – I was a bit worried after everything that happened – and you weren't there. They haven't seen you for a long time.'

'Oh.' I shove myself deeper into the settee and wish the Anglepoise would stop flickering. *Where do I start?*

'So where were you?'

The light bulb breaks with a tiny pinging sound, and we're plunged into darkness. Pa curses and turns on the main light, which floods the room in a cold glare.

'I went back to the house.'

'You made a *promise*, Clem.'

He looks about a year older already, and I haven't even started.

'I'm sorry.'

'Is that it?'

'I had to go back; there was somebody trapped in there.'

'Who? Who was trapped in there?' He scuttles forward on his chair.

'Someone from school. A boy . . . I saw him there the first time, but I ran away from Ganymede before I could get him out, so I had to go back, Pa – I had to!'

Hot tears flood down my cheeks, and Pa abandons his chair, dropping down on to the settee and holding me tight.

'I'm sorry,' I say. 'I didn't think it would be so difficult.'

'What happened in there?' he asks, pulling away and staring at me.

'I saw Ganymede again, and I got away from her and I found Dylan, but then Io was there, and she's even worse than Ganymede, and so we had to run. We ran away. Neither of them even knew who I was, Pa! They didn't know me at all . . .'

'Your mother didn't want them to know,' he says. 'She didn't want you to get caught up in it all.' He sighs and shakes his head, and even the air around us feels heavy.

'But I *am* caught up in it all,' I say fiercely. 'And I can't promise I won't go back, because it's part of me.'

'Part of you?'

'The magic that's in the house – Ma's magic . . .' I take a deep breath. 'I think she's there, Pa.'

'What?' He bolts forward.

'I think she's in the house. It's not a normal house – there are thousands of places she could be. So I need to go back and find her.'

'You think she's been trapped there all this time?'

'I don't know.'

'I knew it wasn't a normal house,' he says. 'But I always thought that if she was in there it would be because she *wanted* to be.'

'Maybe.' I shrug. 'I don't know for sure that she's even in there. But if there's a chance . . .'

He stares at me, and there's a full-on battle happening inside him; I can see it there in his face.

'You shouldn't go back,' he says, but he doesn't mean it. I've never seen his eyes gleam like that before.

'It'll be OK,' I say. 'I can't pretend it isn't happening, and I don't want to go around zapping people in class either, so I have a plan.'

'A plan?' He shakes his head, incredulous. 'What on earth are you going to do *next*?'

'I'm going to go back, and ask Ganymede to teach me.'

'What?' He bounces up, hits his head on the light, sending shadows spiralling into the corners. 'No you're not!'

'It'll be OK,' I say, too tired to argue properly. 'She's not going to hurt me, and while I'm there I can look for Ma.'

'I don't trust her, Clem. I don't know about any of this . . .'

'Do you trust *me*?'

'You're twelve, Clementine! It isn't a question of trusting you . . .'

He hasn't said no, I realize. Not yet.

'Maybe we can talk about it more in the morning,' I say. 'When we've had time to think?'

He sighs, and I pull myself out of the settee and rush to the door before he has the chance to find more difficult words.

'I'm going to get something to eat,' I say.

'Make sure some of it is *green*,' he shouts out after me as I head to the kitchen.

I make myself a ham sandwich and find a bag of crisps with green on the packet. Then I eat an orange because I feel guilty. The wedge of my mother's ruined book is in my back pocket, and I know I should be making a plan to get back in there, but I can't focus enough. The day clamours in my mind in a whirl of feathers and butterflies and snow and unfamiliar faces. I think about the old woman, and the hints that there's someone in there who looks like me. Then I fall asleep at the table and dream of tiny fluttering birds that look a little like books, until Pa wakes me with a tut and makes me go to bed.

16

Once I'm in bed, it's hard to get back to sleep, even though I'm more exhausted than I thought possible. After what feels like hours of tossing and turning, I drag out the head torch and pick up my mother's book, stained and battered, the gold-edged pages crinkled and stuck together. I hold it between my hands and picture the house in my mind, calling on my magic to somehow restore what was there before. My palms grow warm as a pale golden light breaks out around me. A thrill rushes through me at the now familiar feeling, and when the moment is over, I open the book eagerly.

It doesn't look the same. There's the sketch of the house, only now there is colour in it, and the dark, shaded lines that bordered the steps are trailing vines of flowers. The writing is more evenly spaced, the pages somehow clearer, and when I start to read I feel like I'm really seeing what she actually wrote for the first time. Like all the times before there was something obscuring it.

I don't know where we are going, these days.

Ganymede is more strict than ever since our parents died, and I can see that it is done out of fear, and love, but it feels like being in a trap, sometimes. Io rebels harder than I do; she is determined to cause mischief with the globes. And the harder Gan fights for control, the harder Io pulls back. Her heart is huge, her capacity for rage even bigger, and she sends whole storms through the snowglobes just to irritate Gan – I feel so sorry for the poor souls inside!

That is the trouble, I think. I do not agree that magic should be trapped away in these glass globes. There is both good and bad in it, as in everything, and a huge number of people have a little *magic, if not so much as we are blessed – or cursed – with. Half the world could end up trapped in this little house if they carry on like this.'*

I cannot put the book down. It's like I've struck a vein. With every page, I know her more, I understand more of what has happened in that house, and why my aunts are the way they are.

The three of them were alone in that house for years after the deaths of their parents. The place had started life as a small school, set up by their father's mother when her own magic and that of her children became troublesome. The school grew and grew as magic spread among the growing population of the world, and by the time the sisters' parents took over, it was cracking at the seams.

Their mother developed the snowglobes: little worlds where magic could make illusion seem real, where magicians could be free of the burden of trying to conceal or control their power. They discovered that time moved differently in those worlds, that what seemed a dozen years in there could be a day in the real world, and so when pupils were unruly they were put inside – just for a day or a week – and prevented from returning home. Gradually the time got longer; gradually more and more of the magicians were put inside. It was easier, and it seemed to keep the real world safe.

By the time the parents died, they had instilled in their daughters the notion that all magic was dangerous, that all magicians should be contained. When their responsibility was handed to the three sisters, each was to play their own part in maintaining that delicate balance. But Ganymede took more than her share of responsibility. She lived like a recluse, rarely going out and using her power to keep them protected from the outside world, a spell around the house that meant they would always be hidden and self-sufficient.

She collected books on magic and taught her younger sisters more about their craft, always warning of the consequences of using it recklessly. But, as they got older, Io instead sought the wisdom and the company of the entrapped magicians, regularly going into the globes to learn more about their ways and developing a bond with their worlds. Unable to challenge her powerful sister, she sought freedom within.

I flick through the book, marvelling at all the beautiful coloured sketches of the globes – there is even a picture of the fox! And then, towards the back, the writing gets smaller, the tone is different, as if ages have passed.

For so long, it was home, that place. I found comfort in the gardens, and that was where I used my power, beneath Ganymede's careful eye. But it was so lonely! When I saw Piotr, with his flame-red hair, I could not resist saying hello. We talked, day by day, while I tended my garden, and there was such kindness in his eyes, such love for the world in his stories. The house began to feel like a trap. Ganymede's silver eyes followed me wherever I went, and Io's own eyes had already turned towards the magical worlds in the globes.

One day, I followed him out of the garden and through the gate, my feet barely touching the ground for fear Ganymede would stop me. And oh, what he showed me – what joy there was! I could not go back, could not unsee what I had seen, could not abandon the life that beckoned so sweetly.

I did return to them once, just a few weeks later. I barely found the house myself, and when I entered the air was dust, and Io nowhere to be seen. Ganymede was a swish and a tumble of icy wrath – without me, I suppose there was nobody to bridge the gap between them. Io had retreated for good into the worlds of the magicians, and every inch of that house was a *prison — a beautiful, sparking prison of swirling globes.*

I tried to reason with Ganymede, but she was full of a quiet, hard rage against us both. She pledged that any who showed a sign of magic would end up in one of those worlds, and I fled, for there was no more mercy there.

These later pages of my mother's diary are scrawled and tear-stained, the ink driven deep into the paper. She grieved for her sisters, even as she found light in the outside world, and life with Pa. It's hard to read it, hard to stay angry with her, when I can see right here in the press of the pen strokes how much we meant to her. How unlikely it was that she would have just walked out. Somehow, I think, her sisters got her back. Somehow, they have kept her.

I close the book and hold it close.

She is there, somewhere. I have to go back. I know it now even more than I did before.

17

'Clem! There's someone here for you,' Pa calls out in the morning, while I'm testing the static between my fingers to see if I can make things move with my mind.

I can't.

'You're a bit wild around the eyes,' Pa says, pinging the door open and craning his head round. 'What are you doing?'

I sit up. 'I've been reading Mum's book. Who's here?'

He gives me a long hard look, as if there are a lot of things he wants to say and he's not sure how to say them. 'Dylan –' he comes into the room, closing the door behind him – 'is he the reason you went back in? Is he the boy you rescued?'

I nod, wondering where this is going.

Pa runs a hand through his hair. 'It was very

headstrong of you, to go marching back into that house,' he says, folding his arms. 'And I am *not* happy that you lied to me.'

'I'm really sorry,' I say.

'It was also brave.' He sighs, staring at me, sitting at the foot of the bed. 'And the sort of thing your mother might have done. So I've got this for you . . .' He pulls something from his pocket. 'She made it when you were born. She planned to give it to you when you were sixteen, but I'd like you to have it now. Perhaps it will give you some protection. I know she put some of her magic into it.' He hands me a ring made of gold and silver twisted together, a red stone at its centre.

I take the ring and stare at it. It's warm in my fingers, and the gleam of the stone is soothing – like firelight on a cold night.

'Callie was pretty careful, Clem,' he says, standing. 'I want you to be careful too. And I want you to tell me when you're going there. And no more lies.'

'OK,' I say, when I can trust my voice, sliding the ring on to my right index finger. 'Thanks, Pa.' I give him a tight hug, and hope it says everything I can't find the words for right now.

*

'How do you know where I live?' I ask Dylan, when Pa has let himself out with a little backward look and a whispered, *'Be careful – remember . . .'*

'Mum was talking about it – the street, the balcony . . . it wasn't hard to find. Maybe I used magic? I don't know; everything's a bit of a blur. We have to go back for Helios,' he says in a rush. He looks feverish, and I'm kind of surprised his mum let him out at all.

'We will,' I say, leaning back against the radiator, enjoying the creep of warmth up my back. I'm so tired, and just the sight of him makes me feel even more weary. We have to go back – he's right. But just one look at him and I know we can't – not yet. Besides, I have a plan.

'Now,' he says.

'Dylan, if we go in like this, we're just going to get trapped. We'll never get past my aunts and, even if we did, how will we find Helios? How will we find my mother? I'm scared we'll end up locked in there. You were there for a day, and look what it did to you.'

He looks down at himself. 'I thought I wasn't doing too badly.'

'Well, you look terrible. You should go home.'

'And just go back to normal?' he demands, his eyes

glittering. 'After all that, just go back home, go to *school* on Monday? Is that what you're going to do?'

'No, I'm going back to the house. I'm going to get Ganymede to trust me, and teach me how to use magic properly, while I search the house for the globes my mother and Helios are in. And when I've found them we'll go back and get them out.'

He stares at me for a long time, and I smile, trying to look like I've got it all under control. I know it's the right thing to do; it just doesn't feel that way. I can sense the impatience in him, the buzz of needing to do something *right now*, and my own blood sings with the need to get back in there. But we can't. We're not strong enough.

'No,' he says finally. 'I'm going back to that house. Now.' And he bangs out of the door.

I grab my coat and fly after him, nearly falling down the steps, because he's sitting halfway.

'What are you doing?' I shout, grabbing the banister.

'I don't know.' He sighs.

I take a deep breath and sit next to him. 'I swear to you, we will get back in there. We'll get them out.'

'You say it like you think it's going to be easy.'

'No,' I say. 'I told you, I'm going to make sure we're

151

prepared. We have magic, and we can use it when we're in there, but only when you're better. Only when we know where we're going!'

He sighs and pulls himself up, holding on to the banister and looking like an old man on his last legs.

'I don't like it.'

'I don't like it either! I don't like any of it. I want Helios out of there as badly as you do, Dylan!'

'And your mother?' He stares at me.

'Yes. Her too.'

He sighs again, and the fire goes out of his eyes. For now. 'Will you be at school on Monday?'

I've absolutely no idea how I'm going to make that happen, but I can't bear the thought of him walking in there like this, everyone expecting him to be just as he usually is. Jago will see it immediately, surely? He was so quick to see it in me. Maybe if I talk to Mrs Duke, she'll let me off. I can try, anyway.

'I'll be there,' I say, and he turns and hobbles away.

18

I'm standing at the bus stop waiting for Dylan, huddled into my coat and trying to ignore the fact that I'm not supposed to go to school at all today. I've been practising what I'm going to say to Mrs Duke, about how sorry I am and how it'll never happen again. I can't believe I'm really going to do this, especially for a boy who just stood there for so long while I got picked on. Maybe that's why – because I know what it's like to go in every day feeling like an outsider, and doing it anyway.

Now I have somebody who understands, so even if I'm still different, more different than I was before, it won't matter, because so is he. I grin when he comes tearing round the corner, just as the bus arrives in a pile of icy slush, bag flapping, coat hanging off his shoulders.

'Do you feel better?' I ask as we clatter up the steps.

'Ngh,' he says, tucking himself into the back row, drawing his coat tight and slumping into the patterned seat. 'I'm OK.'

'I've been thinking about my ma, and Helios . . . I thought maybe I'd pop into town after school, see if I can talk to Ganymede.'

'Helios . . . yeah,' he says with a whisper of a smile. 'Good idea.'

But there's no spark in his eyes. He looks out of the window, and I chatter on for a bit about the book, and my chat with Pa, but he hardly seems to hear me. It's no wonder he's distant after everything that happened, I suppose. I remember how alone he was in that world where I found him. How we ran from place to place, caught in the wonder and danger of it all, how we used our magic to pull ourselves through. I twist the ring on my finger, and the fire-gleam warms me. I know the adventure isn't over yet, and we're still connected, because apart from anything else we both want to get Helios back.

But, in spite of all that, the bus is cold, and as we get closer to school, more kids get on, and it starts to feel like any other day. Maybe none of what we went through really matters here at all. The more I think it, the longer he keeps his face turned from mine, the smaller I get, until we pull up outside the school, and I feel just the same as I always did: hopeful and stupid all at once.

My heart sinks when I see Jago waiting by the gate with a couple of his friends. They look up when the bus doors open, and Dylan scrambles past me while I'm still trying to pick up my bag, rushing down the steps and making his way over to them. By the time I get off the bus, they're heading to the main doors.

'*Dylan!*' I call.

The red bead in my new ring flashes with my frustration, and Dylan turns, his cheeks flushed, eyes sparking. Jago and the others watch with narrowed, curious eyes as I charge up the path and he doesn't move; he stays right there with his *friends*. I should just turn round and walk away, I tell myself. I should just go home and try to find a way to get back into the snowglobes. But I don't even slow, because I can't. I fought my way back to this world because this is where I belong. And, if I hadn't done that, Dylan wouldn't be here either.

'Well, I thought you'd been suspended,' Jago says with a nasty little smile as I get close. 'What are you doing here?'

'She's fine,' Dylan says, standing between us.

A flare of hope goes through me.

'We talked on the bus; she's not so bad.' He smiles at me, though the smile never reaches his eyes. 'You should go and find your friends.'

I stare at him. I can't breathe, can't swallow. I just stand there, and they laugh at the shock on my face. Dylan doesn't laugh; he just gives me that sorry, pitying smile. And that's even worse. How is this happening?

'You're a coward,' I say, and my voice thrums with anger and the power that I spent the weekend building, for us. So we could go back and get Helios. 'Standing there with them like nothing ever happened.'

Jago frowns. 'What happened, Dylan? What's she talking about?'

'I don't know,' mutters Dylan, shuffling his feet. 'Come on, let's go inside.'

Jago stares at me, his eyes full of hate. 'You're a *freak*.' He spits it, and I can see behind the sneer that he's afraid of me. 'Get out of here,' he snarls. 'And, if I were you, I'd stay away.'

I stand my ground, but the bell goes, and kids swarm around me, pushing and shoving. I watch as they turn away from me, and Jago and Dylan head up the stairs together. I really thought it would be different today. I was going to beg with Mrs Duke to let me in, just so I could be there for Dylan, but he doesn't need me at all. Heat prickles my skin, and the ring glows, fire-bright and full of danger. I can't stay here. There's nothing to stay for anyway.

After a while, I start walking back to town, and the snow turns into fine, icy rain that stings my face and turns the slush to puddles. I'm going to find the house. I'm going to find it, and I'm going to make my aunt Ganymede teach me everything she knows about magic, and then I'm going to wage war in those snowglobes and get my mother out of there.

I don't need Dylan to do that. I don't need anyone.

19

Be there, be there.

Every footstep, pounding like my heartbeat in my ears. *Be. There. Be. There.* And then, as I turn the corner, I add a big sparking roar of *PLEASE* . . . and there it is. Stretching to the sky, a shard of bone against all the grey dark of the houses that have built up around it over hundreds of years. The house they built with all their cursed magic.

I stomp up the steps, my mother's ring a blinding spark at my side, and sweep the door open with a single gesture to find Ganymede waiting for me on the other side, halfway down the stairs. *I am not afraid of her*, I tell myself, stepping into the echoing house, looking her square in the eye. *I am not. I can do anything she can do.*

Probably.

'You're back,' she says, sounding very unimpressed, sweeping down the grand staircase, amid all the flickering lights, lace fluttering as she comes towards me. She tilts her head, a mechanical movement that reminds me she's not really very human at all.

Was she ever?

I open my mouth, find my voice deep down and dark. 'I need you to teach me.' The words seem to bloom in the air, and the snowglobes around us begin to stir.

Ganymede raises an eyebrow. 'Teach you?' she demands, and a single moth descends from the hazy light of the chandelier to spiral over her head. 'You got in and out of my prisons all by yourself – I don't even know how you did that – why do you need *my* help?'

'I want to go back. I left something there.'

'And what is that?' She looms over me, a tower of strange magic and mystery, her grey eyes wolfish, hungry.

'I'm not telling you.'

'You're not telling me,' she says with a whisper of a smile on her face. 'I see. And if I refuse to teach you?'

'Then you'd be even more evil than I thought you were,' I say defiantly.

She steps back with a crack in her facade, rare colour flushing her cheeks.

'You know I'm Callisto's daughter – are you really going turn me away?'

'I don't know anything about you, child.' She shakes her head, flapping a hand at me, and looks surprised when I don't immediately scurry away back down the steps.

'Yes you do. Are you afraid?'

'No!' She strides past me and whacks the door closed with a touch of her hand, before turning back to me. 'Not that I need to explain myself to you, but this place is dangerous for an untrained young girl, whoever she is, and I'm not about to put this house, or all of the worlds here, in jeopardy. Not if I have any choice about it!'

'Why don't you just let them all go?' I gesture at the globes, where solitary figures stand frozen while storms rage around them. Glittering sands and ice-cold snow, tossing and turning, settling on upturned noses, gathering in the crook of a tiny arm. I shiver. I know how that feels.

'No,' Ganymede says with a frown. 'That is quite impossible.'

'Why?'

'Because they're dangerous!' she says. 'You've encountered some of them presumably, on your little adventure – do you think they belong out there in your world?'

'I don't know. I know they don't belong in there forever. Have you ever been in there yourself? Do you know what it feels like?' I point to a world where the girl still sits on her church steps, stars spiralling in all directions as she cups her face in her hands, her shoulders rounded.

She frowns, looking from the girl to me. 'I have always been in control of my power, little snippet,' she says. 'And, when it comes down to it, you don't know much at all yourself. How you tripped through those worlds and came out again in one piece, I can only imagine. Sheer luck. I expect the storms are worse in there now because you've angered Io, stealing one of her treasures . . .'

'Her *treasures*? Do you mean Dylan? He's not a treasure – he's a boy!' *And an awful, treacherous one at that*, I think savagely, pointing all my anger at her.

'He must have a little magic,' she says.

'So what?' I demand.

'Magic is dangerous; it doesn't belong out there. That is what our family does, Clementine. We protect your safe little world from the tumult of magic. What you see in those globes is there so that it does not happen outside!'

I bite my lip and stare at her. She stares back.

'So teach me,' I say, my voice shaking as I try to bring it under control. 'Teach me, so that I can help you. So that I don't cause trouble out there.'

'Perhaps you don't belong out there at all,' she says, looking me up and down, her eyes impassive. 'You are a rush of emotion. Even now it makes the air thick. What happened to you?'

'I grew up without a mother.' I throw it at her, satisfied when she flinches. 'I didn't know about this place. I didn't know about magic. I just thought I was weird. And then when I got here I saw a boy from school, so I went in and I fought against Io to rescue him, and now he won't even look me in the eye.' I'm not sure I meant to say the last bit. I try to unwind myself before she really does throw me out, and end with a whisper: 'And it's lonely.'

'Yes,' she says, after a long silence, looking me up and down. 'Loneliness I understand. Years of nobody and nothing, of time passing while you sit and watch the world go by.'

'So . . . will you teach me?'

She sighs, folding her arms with a rustle of silk and pewter. 'I am not a good teacher. I lack patience.'

'I'm not a baby.'

A haunted look flashes across her face. She takes a step closer to me, and for a moment I think she's going to reach out. 'No,' she says finally. 'No you're not. And there is a likeness . . . Can she really have had a child and not told me?' She takes a deep breath and turns a full circle, taking in all the swirling worlds, all the tiny figures trapped within, and when she comes back to me her mind is set. 'You can start in Callisto's garden. That is where her magic found its best home, the earth itself taught her much. Prove to me that you have her ability; prove to me that you are really kin.'

'But it's . . . it's a monster!'

'It is,' Ganymede agrees, looking out of the window, where brambles cling close. 'I let it go when she left to be with that boy. I shouldn't have; it was small of me. Now that you're here, you can fix it. I'll make some Bovril tea in a while, and if you have shown some ability, I will consider teaching you.'

'Bovril?'

'It's warming,' she says. 'You'll be needing it by the time you finish out there. Callisto always liked Bovril. Come with me.'

I do not know what Bovril is, but it sounds pretty gruesome to me. I slip down the icy steps with her and look with despair at the enormous brambles and forests of things with thorns growing from the under-growth.

'Why am I doing this?' I ask myself, as Ganymede brings out a heavy metal box with rusted hinges and hands it over to me. It's cold out here, and the light is leeching from the world as thick clouds gather.

'Because you say you want to learn,' she says, gesturing at the wilderness. 'And this is where you start.' She sweeps back up the steps, and the door closes with a boom that shakes the ground.

I sit at the bottom and open the box. Inside are bright tools: shining copper trowels and spades, little packets of seeds, coils of wire. I dig through and find some beautiful, brutal-looking shears, and stare at the brambles for a while. They twist from the ground to the marble steps and claw their way up to the front of the house. When I attack with my shears, they attack back, thorns stabbing into my hands as the twisted vine whips out to get me.

I've never really done gardening before. Pa looks after the climbing things on our balcony. I like it when he's out there; it's the only time I ever hear him sing. It's a strange song, which tangles on the tongue and tastes like the wind.

> *Live for me, thrive for thee*
> *'Neath a golden sky, my sweet.*
> *Give my hands, give my love*
> *Into the earth, so . . . Grow!*
> *Fight back the thorns and the monsters, my sweet,*
> *Find the tears of the dawn.*
> *Live for me, thrive for thee*
> *'Neath the love of my hands.*

I start to hum the tune under my breath. I am not going to be beaten by the thick black brambles. When I see that beneath them are stunted trees, pale things bent over and choked by the tangling vines, I work even harder. The sun breaks through the clouds, and after a while I realize I'm singing the song, and it gets easier as the vines stop fighting back. The words twist in the air, the ring on my finger gleams and the little trowel shines bright. The dark place by my heart where a mother might be gets a bit warmer as I fall further and further into the words of the song, and the flash of the copper slashes against all the gnarly roots. Magic curls from my hands and, when I look up what feels like hours later, Ganymede is sitting on the top step in the sun, her grey eyes shining.

The song stutters, the world comes crashing back around me. I was supposed to be searching the house for my mother, or at least learning magic – what am I doing?

'Continue,' she says in her dry voice. 'The spell is working.'

'The spell?'

'Your mother's song. Please. Sing it.'

And I do. I sing, and the vines untwist, the brambles pull easy from the warm soil, and Ganymede tips her head back and looks up at the sky, and just for an instant she could almost be a young girl again, dreaming. Then a cloud covers the sun, and the moment is gone – the iron falls back over her face.

'Come,' she says sharply, standing and looking me up and down.

I'm suddenly aware of the mud on my knees, of how tall and grand she is, and how small I am. My magic has squirreled away for now, deep and dark, leaving only a cold breeze and dirty hands.

'It's time for a break.'

The kitchen is less of a kitchen, more of a clutter. Heavy old ledgers, notebooks and piles of paper have been stacked on to every surface, where they vie with teapots and jars of utensils, groaning spice racks and jars full of mysterious and strange-coloured things. Ganymede reaches for one: a large jar full of thick brown sludge, which is nestled into a corner of the windowsill next to the globe where Timothy presides over his miniature library, sitting cross-legged on the top rung of his tiny ladder, yellow dust drifting down as he shifts to stare at me.

'I did what you asked,' I say, turning from him.

'You began, little snippet.' She shrugs. 'You are not done.'

'But I didn't come here to do your gardening!'

'And yet you will,' she says. 'Your magic is like one of those pale trees out there: it does not know itself yet. It has hardly begun to grow. If you are who you say you are, then you are family, and so I will give you this chance. I will teach you, if you continue your work out there. But you must abandon your idea of getting back into the globes; that is not your place, not unless *I* decide it.'

I stare at her, and she stares back. She does not expect me to question her, I realize. Was this what it was like for my mother and Io? Was she always so sure that she was right? My mind whirrs as I try to work out how I'm going to get what I need out of this. The gardening is strangely intoxicating, but I don't have all the time in the world. I cannot afford to fall under Ganymede's spell and stay here forever; I have to get back in there. I have to find a way to explore the house without her knowing.

As long as she trusts me, it might just be possible.

'For now,' I say. 'If you tell me things.'

'What *things*?' she demands impatiently.

'How do you decide who is locked in a snowglobe?' I ask. 'How did you end up with a whole house full of them? Doesn't it creep you out?'

'Creep me out?' She smiles, shaking her head and turning to light the stove beneath a battered tin kettle with flick of a long finger and a flash of her eyes. 'Our family has always maintained them. The world out there is not easy for one with magic, and magic itself is no good for the world. My grandmother's idea for a school was flawed, and they soon realized it. There was too much power in her students, too much disobedience. So those who abused their powers were locked away, and there they remain. Time passes differently, and they are magicians. They make much of their worlds; they do not suffer.'

'They are all under Io's spell,' I say. 'Most of them are, anyway. And they're not happy in there; they're just enchanted. Why does she stay in there?'

'That is her realm. This is mine,' Ganymede says shortly. 'She prefers to avoid responsibility.'

'Weren't you all supposed to work together to look after it?' I ask.

She narrows her eyes.

'I read it in my mother's book,' I say. 'And Io said you were the one who locked them all away. Which means you put Dylan in there too. Why not me?' I bite my lip; my words keep escaping. I'm supposed to be acting all nice and compliant, and then the anger bursts out.

'He is a boy with untrained power and a reluctance to take responsibility for it.'

'So you just locked him away?' I demand, even while I'm feeling the truth of her words.

'And you released him. We are even in that, at least,' she snaps, pouring steaming water into two china cups with glinting golden rims.

'He thought he was in there for months. It messed him up,' I say.

'He should have been more careful.'

'What did he do? Something with a raindrop – it can't have been that bad!'

'Oh! And you know that, do you, with all your twelve years of magical wisdom?' She cackles darkly. 'No, little snippet, you barely know how to walk. Even playing with raindrops is dangerous if you don't think about the consequences. Now drink your Bovril, and then you should go. You may come back tomorrow and continue your work.'

I take a sip of the steaming brown stuff and try not to spit it straight back out again. It tastes like beef juice, and I suspect that's exactly what it is. Ganymede watches with a sharp eye, as if just waiting for me to prove I'm not magic enough for beef juice or whatever, and so I swallow it and smile.

20

'Why aren't you at school?' Ganymede asks the next morning, when I turn up early. Birdsong followed me all the way here, and cut off as soon as I came through the gate, which was eerie and not at all comforting. It doesn't matter, I tell myself. I can put up with a lot if it means I can find my mother and Helios without having to travel through thousands of worlds under Io's control.

'I have a couple of days off,' I say as she stands aside to let me into the house. The snowglobes roar around us, whorls of water and tiny silver fish splashing up against the glass sides, and I frown. 'What's going on with them?'

'A storm,' she says dismissively. 'Io has a temper; you must have discovered that when you were inside. She's not a morning person. Now tell me about these days off. I didn't think that was how school worked. Is it a *half-term?*' She says the words through her teeth, like they're in a foreign language she still hasn't mastered, narrowing her eyes.

'Uh, no. I got banned for a couple of days.'

'Banished!' Her eyes glitter. 'For what?'

'I pushed someone,' I say, still looking at the globes out of the corner of my eye. 'And they went further than I thought they would. Really, is there something wrong in there? Is it because Dylan and I escaped?'

'There are consequences to everything,' she says. 'As you know. She'll settle down. I suppose you used your power on this boy? That is strictly forbidden, Clementine. You should have been more careful.'

'I didn't mean to! Nothing like that had ever happened before. And now you're teaching me it'll be OK.'

'Will it?'

'I don't know,' I say. 'But you don't need to be locking me away in there. I'd just come back out again, anyway.'

'You might,' she concedes, pursing her lips. 'Though you might find it harder than you think, if you're not the one who puts you *in* there. Callisto was always hopeless at controlling herself – that's why the garden is so wild,' she says. 'Get on with clearing it, and when you come back in, I'll give you a lesson while you have your Bovril.'

She turns her back and swooshes away, Portia winding around her skirts. The door slams, and I turn slowly, looking out over the town, thinking how strange it is that I can see everything from here, and nobody stops to notice this place. They pass by without looking up; not even a stray leaf ever crosses the boundary.

Were the three of them really here for hundreds of years, before Pa showed up and changed everything? Did my ma let him see it, because she was intrigued by him? It would explain why he never saw it again; why he still can't now. As far as I know, Pa doesn't have his own magic. I try to imagine what it was like for her, living here, but it's impossible. I find the world fairly intense most of the time, and sometimes I'm not really sure I belong at all, but I *want* to belong, somewhere . . .

I hold on to that thought as I start to dig at the ground for the roots of the weeds that have choked this place for so long, and the song rises up, warm and stirring, filling my chest. My freezing hands slip on the little trowel that seems no match at all for the job, and the earth is hard as ice around the roots, but when I finally sit back to look, every muscle aching, you can definitely see I've been here. It's not pretty, exactly – the bare places look scarred, and the stunted trees and plants are still pale and scrawny – but it's progress.

Ganymede doesn't show the slightest bit of appreciation when she comes out to get me. 'Lunch,' she says, sweeping back into the house, feather cloak trailing behind her. I follow at a distance, and my skin feels tight because somehow I have to find a way to get away from her to explore the house today, despite all her hawk eyes and moth-fluttering. I'm back at school tomorrow, and I have to have done something before then.

I wish I'd brought a cheese sandwich. Lunch is probably cow-brain spaghetti, or something.

'Concentrate!' Ganymede shouts at me an hour later, after a reasonably normal soup that I'm hoping was tomato.

We're still in the kitchen, and I'm supposed to be keeping my focus while she darts about me like a crazed moth-dragon, roaring and stomping, bashing pans and muttering spells under her breath. Every so often, shadows gather at the corner of my eye, or light flares and the room shakes. Tiny fluttering forms gather at the nape of my neck, and I'm supposed to ignore it all and stand still.

'Is this really necessary?' I ask, trying not to stagger back beneath a barrage of blue sparks coming at me. Her hands are like claws, outstretched towards me, her eyes hard as flint.

'You told me you wanted to learn control,' she says. 'If you cannot find it, I will have to take measures. So you should concentrate. And stop fantasizing about getting back into those globes – I've seen your eyes wandering. Why is it still on your mind?'

'We left our dog in there,' I say. 'I want to get him back.'

Her eyes widen. 'A dog? You'd risk everything for a dog?'

And for a mother, I think.

'Wouldn't you, for Portia?' I demand, my eyes flicking towards the green-eyed cat, who is licking butter from the dish on the kitchen table.

Ganymede doesn't have an answer for that she just throws a colander. I see it bowl towards me, gleaming in the winter sun, turning as it comes my way. I put up a hand to stop it knocking me out, and it halts in mid air, held between us by some force I can't name. It clatters to the floor, dented.

'Not bad reflexes,' Ganymede says. 'How do you feel?

'Fi-ine,' I stutter, finding the edge of the table behind me and leaning against it.

'Tired?'

'Yes.'

'You were fighting me,' she says. 'Your strength against mine. And I wasn't holding back too much, so you did well.'

'Oh good,' I breathe.

'Now, we should work on control. Raise the colander, keep it there, and don't make any more dents.'

It takes a long time to get the colander off the ground. For a moment, it hovers around Ganymede's ankles, and then in a burst of frustration I flick it up into the air, and the whole thing folds like origami.

'What happened?' I exhale.

'Too much force,' she says. 'Like taking a hammer to it. Probably fairly similar to what happened at your school. You need to do things carefully, let it out slowly. Not get frustrated.'

She reaches for the squashed colander and sighs.

'Can't you fix it?' I ask.

'With a hammer, yes.' She turns and starts riffling through drawers.

Timothy stares out at me from the top of his ladder, while yellow flecks of dust fall around his shoulders. He makes a rude gesture, and I remember being there. I remember breaking those doors down, running away from him with Dylan and Helios. I remember how it felt to be part of their team. And if Dylan isn't going to fight for his dog, then I will.

I dash from the room while Ganymede's back is turned, silent as I can, knowing it's the wrong moment, but there's no choice. My eyes flick up and down the shelves as I run, past world after spinning world, just hoping I'll spot a tiny golden dog. I don't look for my mother; I don't know how I'd feel if I suddenly saw her. Would I even recognize her? Is she really here somewhere, just waiting to be discovered? It feels impossible that she could be so close after all this time, so I just focus on Helios, knowing that when I find him we can look for her together.

I dash through room after room where the sun sparks through grimy windows, into dark cupboards where cobwebs hang thick as curtains, and then I hear her behind me. A rustle of movement, a screech that makes my ears pop. My ring flashes on my finger, getting warmer as I flee up a back staircase, and then I'm in a narrow corridor, the walls lined with dark wood shelves, where the globes are yellowed with age, the people in them long-forgotten. Tiny figures rush up to the glass as I fly past them, and Ganymede's footsteps thunder through the house. It's too late for pretending, too late to act the innocent, so I just keep going.

After a while, I realize the figures are heckling in thin, whispered voices, urging me onward, crying for freedom. 'I'm trying. I'm trying,' I hiss at them, bounding up more steps, looking all the time for Helios.

She catches up with me as I reach the carpeted landing at the top of the house, before the tower room where I first found Dylan. She has come up the main stairs and appears before me, wraith-like and furious as the wildest ocean storm.

'I trusted you!' she bursts. 'I let you in! I even tried to *teach* you, and you have betrayed me already! I should have known you would: your father was a thief; he took a part of our heart away with him, and nothing was ever the same again!'

'So you took your revenge?' I shout back, knowing

that this is my last chance to get answers from her – she'll never let me in again. 'How could you take her from us? Where is she now?'

'I didn't . . .' She backs away from me into a shadowed corner.

Snowglobes are in uproar all around us, and the air is so cold our breath steams. Cracks start to run up the walls as thousands of tiny fists beat against the smooth glass of their prisons.

'. . . I didn't mean to. I didn't know you existed! I never would have taken a mother from her child!' Tears streak down her hollow cheeks, but as the clamour of the globes intensifies, she steels herself, coming out of the shadows, reaching up to her full height.

'I do not know where she is now,' she says in a ringing voice. 'And I will not have you tear this house down with your anger. So you have a choice, Clementine.' She stalks towards me as I back away, swallowing hard. 'Leave now and never return, or I will find you a permanent home of your own. You cannot be trusted. And, let me tell you now, you will not break free if *I* curse you there. Your father will have lost you *both* forever.'

I stare at her, but all I can see is my pa's bewildered

face when I don't come home. All I can think is that he never got over losing her, and to lose me too might be the end of him. I go to protest, to shout, but the tide has turned. Her power is far greater than mine in this place, and she has nothing to lose.

I close my eyes and tell Helios I'm sorry. That I'll be back when I can creep in of my own will, when I know I can get us out again. And when I open them again I'm on the cold hard pavement in front of the bakery. The house is nowhere to be seen; the old swing creaks as a bitter wind blows.

She won, for today.

'I'll be back!' I shout at the top of my lungs, making a cloud of pigeons break for the sky.

21

I'm still angry when I wake the next morning. I don't know if Ganymede was telling the truth, or if I might have been able to break her curse and get out of whatever snowglobe she put me in with my own magic. But in that moment she was more terrifying than anything I have ever imagined. I comfort myself that choosing Pa was the right decision, but it feels hollow. I should have played along for longer. I should have helped her mend that colander, done gardening until she stopped watching me like a hawk.

I throw back my duvet and slide out of bed, pulling on my uniform and brushing my hair, dreading the day at school. Pa makes pancakes for breakfast, and looks at me as if he knows today is going to be difficult. I came out of my bedroom hard and ready for anything, and his kindness is making it go soft.

'Got everything you need?' he asks as I head for the front door. He's not usually here at this time making pancakes – it's a special occasion.

'I think so . . .'

'Oh! I made you lunch.'

He hands me a plastic box with different compartments. A roll, a banana, some bits of carrot and a little muffin, all in their own areas.

'What?' he asks, when I stare at him.

'You've never done this before,' I say past a lump in my throat.

'Maybe I should have,' he says. 'Better late than never, eh?'

'Yeah.' I smile. 'Thanks, Pa.'

'Go careful today, then,' he says. 'And stay away from that Jago.'

'I will.'

'Clem?'

I look back at him. His hair blazes as the early morning sun leaches through the window, and his eyes are shining.

'I mean it,' he says. 'Don't let him get to you.'

'OK.'

Of course when I get to the bus stop, Dylan is standing there looking like a nice boy who would stand up for a person. Like a boy who could be a friend.

'Hey,' he says, his crooked smile trying to hide the shadows in his eyes.

I stare at him, waiting for him to say something, to explain what happened, even just to ask how it went with Ganymede, whether there's any word on Helios, but he doesn't. He just looks away. *Hey*, indeed. What the heck does he expect? I'm not going back to being part-time sort-of friends; that's a load of rubbish I *don't* need.

When the bus arrives, I rush on and park myself next to one of the year-seven kids – so there's no chance he can sit next to me – and look out of the window the whole way. The sun is low in the pale blue sky, and the shadows of all the houses and trees cut across the road as we swing through town. In and out, in and out of shadow, lurching all the time. A bit like being in one of those snowglobes. It felt simpler when we were in there. Terrifying, but also kind of clear. Keep going, until you find the way out. Keep hold of your friends, or you'll lose them to Io forever.

I don't regret that. I know I couldn't live with myself if I'd left Dylan in there. It's hard enough knowing I've left Helios behind. How can Dylan turn his back on the only friend he had for such a long time? The friend who kept him warm when he had no strength left? I know magic is hard for him, that he blames it for the death of his father, that his mother fled their seaside home to keep him safe – but can he really think it's just going to disappear? Does he think that pushing me away is somehow going to help? I go round and round in circles, and keep coming back to the same question.

How could you abandon Helios?

I shout it, loud as I can in my mind, and there's a little gasp from behind me, so maybe he heard. I hope he did. I hope my voice blasted through all the little walls he's built.

'You OK?' asks the girl next to me, breaking me out of my fury and making me start. She has curly hair that looks like her mum cut it, and freckles across her nose.

'Yes,' I say, trying to smile.

'Only you're crying a little bit,' she whispers. 'Or something . . .'

'Oh!' I swipe at my cheeks, glad that Dylan is sitting up behind us at the back of the bus. 'Uh, thanks.'

'That's OK,' she says, picking up her bag and riffling through it. Her face turns to mine again; it's so bright and friendly. 'Want a tissue?'

'OK.'

She has a little packet with pictures of kittens on it. She pulls one out and hands it to me. 'Mum packed them, just in case. Not that I cry a lot. More like, if the sun is in my eyes, or something.'

'Yeah –' I take the tissue – 'I know what you mean. Thanks.'

'OK,' she says.

And she turns her face to the window, and then we're at school, and she's scrambling past me, waving madly at someone on the outside. I move along with the rest of the crowd, watching her dash out, coat swinging, clattering to meet her friends, and she's got no idea how much her kindness helped. If one person can be like that, others can too. This place is not full of Jagos; I don't have to be afraid of it. This is school. There is *nobody* here I need to be that frightened of.

I clutch the balled-up tissue in my pocket and keep my head up, walking through the gates, past Dylan, ignoring the clamour and the bustle, just focusing on getting inside and up to my form room. I sit somewhere new, and when people file in there are a few looks and whispers, but I ignore them all, and because I've sat in the middle of a row, people are forced to sit around me. I smile at the girls who slide in on either side of me, and they smile back, even if they look a little puzzled.

Ha!

It's an exhausting day. I make myself do all the things I usually don't do. I smile, I sit in all the wrong places, I brazen it all out and even say 'hi' to a couple of people. Mostly they say 'hi' back, even if they look a bit surprised. Jago lurks, like a spiteful cloud. He's worse than ever with all his jibes and mean, tripping feet, but I ignore him, put a shield up, and by the end of the day it's got boring. Someone tells him to shut up when he calls me 'witchy-witch face' in history. I don't know who; I just sit there and concentrate on Miss Olive, and make notes on the Battle of Hastings. I have more important things on my mind, like how I'm going to get into a house that my weird aunt Ganymede will no doubt be hiding from me.

*

I watch for the bus, wishing it would hurry up. My ring has been flashing all day as I've tried to keep all my emotions in check, and I barely trust myself to be around people now. Tension winds through me, making me jumpy, and when Dylan ambles over I have to bite my lip to keep it from spilling out.

'Clem?'

I glare at him. 'What?'

'I'm sorry.'

'You're *sorry*?'

'I shouldn't have done that, yesterday. I should have put Jago straight. I just . . . It's hard for me.'

I look down at the ground. Tiny amber flecks spiral out on the pavement around my boots, and the ring doesn't help. If anything, it seems to amplify the magic I'm trying hard to control.

'Clem?' He follows my eyes. 'What are you doing?'

'You should get away from me,' I say.

'I know you're not going to hurt me,' he says. 'I'm trying to make it right!'

'What is *wrong* with you?' I howl, stamping my foot, cracks appearing in the pavement.

Dylan steps back.

'How can you be so two-faced? How could you act

as if nothing ever happened and stand there with Jago while he called me a freak? How can you abandon Helios like that? Why don't you want to go back and get him out? What are you so afraid of, Dylan?'

He looks tormented, ashen with doubt. 'I don't know!'

A light rain starts to fall, flying into our faces with the twist of the wind. I know I'm not the one making it, and it's not natural either. A couple of steps away, the sun is still shining, casting bars of shadow on to the pavement from the school fence. I stare at him.

'You can't hide from it forever,' I hiss. 'Even now – look around you, Dylan. This isn't natural rain, and I'm not doing it: *you* are!'

'I don't know what to do,' he chokes, taking a breath, letting the storm wash out. 'Mum won't understand; nobody will understand!'

'They don't need to understand,' I say. 'Do you think they'll hate you for it? Your mum won't, and I don't know about Jago, but why should you care? Do you really think he's such a great friend if you can't trust him with who you are?'

'I'm sorry,' he says. 'I didn't want it to be true. I don't want this! It was OK in there, but out here . . .'

'You don't have a choice,' I say. 'Not in that, anyway. But you can choose your friends; I guess you already did. So I'm going to go back to that house without you. I'm going to find my ma.'

'I'll come,' he says. 'I want to find Helios too.'

'No.'

'Why not?'

'Because I don't trust you.' It hurts to say it, and he winces when he hears it, but it's true. I can't go in there with him like this; there's too much in the way.

It's a huge relief when the bus arrives. I take a deep breath and stomp on, sitting myself firmly in the back corner, sighing loudly when Dylan piles in next to me.

'I'm sorry,' he says again after a while.

'It doesn't matter. Just leave it to me. I'll get Helios. It's my family's mess, anyway.'

He stares at me, but he doesn't say anything, and we don't speak after that. We watch out of the window as the bus winds through the streets, and the streetlights come on, shining blearily through the glass. I try to figure out how I'm going to fix it all. There's a big part of me that's furious with Dylan for casting me aside, but I can see how hard this is for him, and I don't know how I'd feel in his shoes. It's hard to imagine it: trying

189

to hide what you are from your mother and your new family. If I ever find my ma, at least I won't have to do that.

The house is hiding and, no matter how hard I glare at the place where I know it should be, it won't appear for me. I try until there are sparks flying, until my eyes are aching, and eventually I head for home, weary and terrified that maybe I'll never be able to fix this. Maybe Ganymede will hide it so tight I'll never find it again.

Pa stares at me when I get home, so I tell him I'm having an early night; I don't want my despair to meet his. I head for my room, but it's hard to sleep. There's too much in my head. I spend most of the night trying to juggle things using magic: pens, books, bunched-up socks and an old watch. I keep going until I can do it without everything flying at the walls of my bedroom, and I tell myself that will be useful, somehow. It will be strengthening my magic so that I can find the house.

When I wake, the sun is shining, and Pa has left for work, but my new lunchbox is full of neat little packages again. It makes me smile. I linger in the kitchen for a while, flicking through my mother's book, wishing our magic was the fairytale sort, where spells would be written in black and white, and the right words would make anything possible. This kind of magic seems to be about feeling and instinct, and I'd do anything for a nice, simple 'here is how you make the house visible' sort of tip.

'Bleurrrgh,' I tell my reflection in the hallway mirror, baring my teeth at myself as I shove my hat on. 'Tonight. I will get into that place tonight. One day of school, and then everything changes for good. I swear.' My eyes flicker with amber shards as I say it, and I know it probably won't change anything, but it does make me feel a bit better.

I grab my lunch and head out, ignoring Dylan at the bus stop and marching on to the bus alone, sitting by my new friend from year seven. She's called Amelia, and she moved to the area to come to the school, so she didn't know anyone before she started. She doesn't seem that fazed by it now, though, and by the end of the journey I'm surrounded by a little gaggle of her friends.

And then Dylan joins me as we get off the bus.

'Hey,' he says.

'Hey.'

He stays by me all the way to the gate, where Jago is waiting, looking between us with a frown.

'What's going on?' he demands.

'Nothing,' Dylan says tiredly. 'She's OK. Just leave it for a day, can't you?'

'No, because she's *not* OK.'

I breathe deep and think of what Ganymede taught me about control, while Jago stares at me, and Dylan looks at his feet.

'Well, this is awkward,' I say after a moment, when I'm sure I can trust my voice. 'I think I'll just head in.'

'Yeah, you do that,' snarls Jago. 'I'll just have a little chat with my friend here, make sure he's OK.'

'I'm fine, Jago,' says Dylan as I head off. 'What's *your* problem?'

I turn back. Jago is small, but he's wiry, and his expression is mean.

'*She's* my problem,' Jago spits, gesturing towards me with another grimace.

I should just walk away, I tell myself – this isn't my battle. But Dylan looks so conflicted. Dark clouds gather over the school as they stare at each other, and a light rain begins to fall. I stare at Dylan, wondering if he realizes he's using his magic.

'Look!' Jago says as the rain gets heavier, just over their heads. 'Right now, Dyl. She's doing it *right now*!'

Dylan looks at me as the rain turns to a torrent around us all. I spread my hands beneath the deluge, telling him in my mind: *It's not me!* He frowns, and I roll my eyes, turning my gaze downwards. Tiny buds begin to worm their way through the cracks in the pavement, and when they open they look just like the flowers in my mother's book. Red petals in a star shape, sparkling amber at their centre. I ignore Jago and grin at Dylan, feeling reckless. *That's me!* His eyes widen, and the rain eases off, the clouds breaking apart, just a few drops carried on the breeze to fall on the new flowers.

'Wow,' he says eventually with a grin as the bell rings and kids start to plough in around us.

'You're *both* sick,' Jago says, his eyes a little wild, looking between us.

'You wish you could make that happen,' Dylan says.

'Nobody should be able to make any of it happen! It's dangerous!'

'No,' Dylan says, stepping closer to him. 'We're not dangerous. *We* know words hurt. *We* know when to stop. *You* should have stopped, a long time ago.'

'She threw me across a classroom!'

'Yes, and then I went away and learned not to do that again!' I burst. 'What about you? What have *you* learned from all the times you made my life a misery?'

'You think I was the only one?' he demands. 'What about your friend Dylan here? Want to hear all the words he used about you?'

'No, thank you,' I say, my heart hammering at the thought, and trying to ignore it. 'I'm not doing this any more. Just leave me alone.'

I stride away, and Dylan comes with me, and I don't know what kind of friendship this is, but he's beside me right now, so I guess that must mean something.

'I never thanked you properly,' he says as we get into the form room. 'For coming into that snowglobe after me . . .'

I shrug. 'It was the right thing to do.'

'So when are we going back?'

'I don't know. I made Ganymede angry.'

'How did you make her angry?'

'I started exploring the house and she caught me. She threatened to put me in a snowglobe, and said that if she was the one who put me in I wouldn't be able to escape again. And then she threw me out.'

'We'll sneak in together,' he says. 'And if she finds us I can always distract her while you get back in.'

'You might get trapped again,' I say.

'Not if I use my magic,' he says in a quiet voice, staring at his hands. 'I mean, I might not get out on my own, but I'd find a way through the worlds. I could find Helios. You could find your mum. And if you got in by yourself you could get us out again. Like you did last time.'

'I don't know,' I whisper as Mr Varley comes into the room. 'You don't need to put yourself in danger. I can probably manage.'

'Let me help,' he says. 'The last few days have been terrible. I need to help.'

'It'll be dangerous,' I say.

'I know that. So is everything else. Could get hit by a bus . . .'

I snort. 'Well, you might, but that's a remote chance. Walking back into a house where you got trapped for months is just asking for trouble.'

'Please?' He stares at me, his eyes wide. 'I'm sorry. I'm so sorry I took it all out on you. I'm sorry I let you face everything on your own. I *swear* to you I'll never let that happen again.'

22

The house is still hiding, but we have a plan. We *know* it's there, and so we carry on as if we can see it. We help each other up the steps, and they keep glimmering and vanishing before our eyes, and it's difficult to walk on something invisible, but we move forward anyway, drawing on our magic to help us see our way.

'Maybe we should close our eyes,' Dylan whispers.

His fingers are wrapped tight round my upper arm, and mine clutch at his shirt. I close my eyes and shuffle forward, moving up when my foot hits the edge of the next step.

'What about when we get into the house, though?' I ask, my teeth chattering.

The whole place is like a fog of ice, a mist that keeps flickering, one moment showing a great tall house that sweeps to the stars, and the next an impossible climb over the old park fence.

'She can't keep the whole place invisible. It'll just be the outside,' he says, not sounding too sure.

'I was hoping at least this first bit would be straightforward—'

I slip on a step, and bite my lip to stop from shouting out as Dylan yanks me back, stopping me from falling into the brambles. We both end up on our knees, half laughing, half howling, tears rolling down our faces as we try not to let any sound escape. We crawl up the steps after that, collapsing with relief when we finally reach the top and the carved marble porch is at least ninety per cent visible, mist swirling over the vast, skin-covered door.

'It's not really skin, is it?' Dylan asks as we press our palms against it, hoping our magic will do the rest of the work and let us in without giving us away to Ganymede. I've been trying to focus on the idea of *us* being invisible, to see if we can use her trick against her. If we can avoid her, this will be all the easier.

'No, it can't be. She probably made it feel that way to discourage people,' I whisper as the door gives beneath our touch, swinging open to reveal the huge entrance hall, shelves covered in snowglobes on every side.

I start forward on tiptoe, hushing the globes as I pass, and I think it's going well until I look around and see Dylan isn't with me.

'Dylan?'

The mist has crept through the door, the hall is quickly clouding up and I can't see him.

'I'm here,' he says. His eyes are hollow with shock; his face slack with it.

'What's wrong?' I ask, pulling him along towards the stairs.

'This place!' he whispers. 'I had no idea how big it is. I barely registered it when we came through before. There are so many, Clem. And they're all prisons? Is there a magician in every single one?'

I nod, trying to get him to the stairs before we're discovered. Apart from anything else, I don't think he'd cope with Ganymede in full-on moth-swish mode right now.

'And you knew all this and you *still* came in to get me . . . You must have known we might never find our way out again!'

'That's why we didn't go straight back after,' I whisper. 'It's fine. We're going to fix it.'

'We are,' he says, as if to convince himself.

You are? comes a tide of whispers, a rumble that strikes at us deep within, as the figures within the globes rush to watch us pass. Somewhere, Ganymede is stirring. I can feel the charge in the air, the snap of tension that builds around her when she's disturbed. A footstep, the query of a far-off voice. Portia prowls past us, and my skin erupts into amber static. Dylan pulls away, wincing, and the globes around us start to turn in a tide of confusion.

We'll sort it, I promise to the sea of tiny faces staring at us from behind the glass globes. *But we can't let Ganymede find us here now. She'll stop us, and we'll never get another chance then. Distract her. Don't let her know we're here!*

'You think you can walk in here and turn them all to your side?' Ganymede demands, flying down the stairs towards us, her eyes sparking. 'You think you can *hide* in my own house?' She cackles, moths swirling in the air around her. 'Silly children; you have walked into the trap all by yourselves.'

'No,' I say.

No! they roar around us.

'What do you mean, *no*?' she demands, looking imperiously from us to the globes as the fog lifts.

You are not the only mistress here, says a tiny single voice, ghostlike in the sudden silence. *The new one is strong, and she does not stand alone, as you do. Maybe she can bring this whole place down. You think we will not help her to that end?*

'Oh, be quiet,' she says, looking down with a frown as Portia winds around her ankles, hobbling her. 'You have no power here: you are prisoners!'

'*We're* not,' Dylan says, standing tall beside me. His voice doesn't quake, his hands don't tremble and his magic is a rush of energy all around him.

'But you were, and you can be again,' says Ganymede, her nostrils flaring.

'Where is she?' I ask, my voice thin.

She stares at me.

'What did you do with her, Ganymede?'

'Nothing,' she says, but she doesn't sound so sure now. New lines appear on her face as cracks rush up the walls of the house. 'I did nothing wrong. Everything I ever did was in pursuit of safety, of keeping things under control!'

'Why did you do it?' I ask, through the hammer of my heart. 'Where did you put her, Ganymede? Where did you lock my *mother*?' It comes out as a screech, full of rage and my own unpredictable magic, and it rings through the house, echoing bell-like off all the glass, reaching to the highest ceiling.

We stare at each other, and I see it in her face: there is no more hiding, no more doubt. Finally she knows I am Callisto's daughter; truly she believes it.

And it shatters her.

She crumples before us, moths fluttering out in every direction, and she doesn't look like Ganymede at all, as she lands at the bottom of the stairs. In this moment she is not tall and strong. She is not beautiful. She is wilted, the iron melting away until she's as scared and as flawed as anyone else.

'I didn't know,' she says, looking at me with eyes awash with tears, as wide and bright as the moon. 'I told you before – I didn't know she'd had a child! She came to me, so tired, so sad. The world out there was brutal to my dearest heart, and I could not bear to see her age, or fade. She was *our* baby, and we both doted on her, and so I put her away to be with Io, to keep her safe for a while. Io must have a hand in this as well, for

I didn't trap Callisto there! I thought she'd come back when she'd gained strength from Io – they were always so close – but she never did. Io must have tricked her, kept her there – and when I went to find her she had gone.'

She stands clumsily, puts a thin hand on one of the banisters. 'I tried to find her! I wanted to bring her out; I'd made such a terrible mistake. But she was not *there. She was not there, Clementine!* What could I *do*?' She sweeps out past us to the globes, peering into one after the other. 'I cannot find her. I do not know where else to look, and I could not leave this house to go in there. Io has hidden her away!'

She carries on searching, her long skirts sweeping the tiles, swirling out around her, fists clenched by her sides, and Dylan grabs my arm as the cracks in the walls begin to multiply, like the new branches on a tree, spiralling out, creeping ever higher.

'We need to get in there,' he says. 'Quickly, before she comes back to her senses. We need to go and find Io, and get her to tell us.'

'I don't know where to get in!' I say, feeling a little like Ganymede, breathless with fear and feelings buried deep for too long.

'Focus,' Dylan says. 'We need to get on the other side of all this.'

'No,' whispers Ganymede. 'No. I cannot let you. I cannot let you loose to enter all these prisons and stir up all these souls. They are content as they are; you will bring chaos!' She stares at us, and begins to mutter to herself. 'The boy, perhaps, can be contained, but Clementine – she is strong as copper. Strong as the sun, and the moon, and the Earth together – strong as any of us. What will she do? What . . .'

Suddenly the air begins to thicken again. With a whisper from the globes, the fog closes in. Ganymede shrieks, and Dylan and I run up the stairs, down corridors where whole worlds call out our names, and up to that attic room. Footsteps come hard after us, and there is no more time, there are no more chances.

I show Dylan where I first found him, and we put our hands against the glass of his globe. My mother's ring glows. A needle flash of bright burning goes through me, Dylan is wrenched away and I'm spinning, flying through the air, landing on the hard ice, my breath caught in my chest. A bleak, cloud-filled sky fills the horizon. A bitter wind riffles through my clothes. I am back in the world where I found him, winded and spooked by everything that just happened.

And there is no house this time. There is no Dylan to stop me slipping down the mountainside. There is no Helios to bound over and warm my feet.

I am alone, snow falling in great folds over me as I crash into the glass barrier, banging my head against the transparent wall that divides me from reality.

23

I watch her fall down the hillside and I know that feeling, I know the way the ice stings, snow clinging in great swathes until you're too cold to think, too cold to move. I know it, even as I watch it happen, even as Ganymede claws me back away from the globe.

'You!' she cries. 'I will keep you, and she will return to me. I will be able to explain.'

'You can't,' I say, pulling away from her. 'You can't keep me, and you can never explain!'

'But I must! She must understand it was for the best, it was for safety, for the world. I put away the magic, and Io was free to rule in there. It was the deal we two made, when Callisto left us. I told her I would never interfere in there, if she left the real work to me. I put Callisto in that day because she needed comfort, and they were always so close.'

She sighs. 'I didn't think Io would keep her there against her will!'

'You *took away Clem's mother, and you left her in there all this time. You didn't check, did you? She hasn't known her for ten years. She doesn't remember how she looks, the smell of her, the way she feels when she holds her . . .' My eyes blur as I think of my dad, of all the times I've imagined us together again. 'You can't* ever *make that better.'*

'I didn't know she had a child! Time means nothing in there. It would have meant nothing to Callisto, except that Clementine has aged, and there is nothing I can do about that! If I put them away together, if I weave magic around them, maybe then . . . maybe they can make it better in there . . . They can build a whole world together. Maybe I can make it right.' She stares from me to the globes around us, as if searching for the perfect place to make a little paradise.

'No,' I say. 'No more hiding. No more pretending. You'll just have to say you're sorry.'

'Say I'm sorry?' Her voice breaks. 'How will that be enough? Clementine is strong – she will find Callisto and, between them, who knows what they might do to this place? They could set free every one of them, and then what?'

'I don't know,' I say. 'You'll have to figure it out.' And I turn back to the globe, just as Clem is rising, slipping on *the ice, as she puts her hands against the glass to catch her balance. I put my hand on the globe and I close my eyes and I go back, back to the place where I lost myself, where I lost hours, and days, maybe months of my life. I go back there.*

But I am not the same now.

I am magic, through and through. And so is she.

24

'Dylan!' I've never been so pleased to see anyone. I rush at him and we go flying into the snow. I feel as if I've been here for hours already, but I know it can't be that long. It was probably just a moment out there.

'What happened?' I ask, scrambling up and brushing the snow off my jumper.

He climbs up slower, avoiding my eye.

'Dylan?'

'Ganymede grabbed me,' he says. 'That's all.'

'No it isn't!'

'OK, well, she also threatened to lock you up with your mother so you could live in some dream where none of this ever happened, and I told her to get lost. And then I got in.'

I stare at him.

'Not that it changes anything,' he says, 'but I've never seen anyone look so guilty before.'

'She—' I burst angrily.

'I know,' he interrupts. He looks tired already. 'I know what she did. I know how it feels to be without someone. I told her so. The good thing is we're here, and we know for sure your mum is here somewhere too.' He shivers, looking around. 'I can't believe I actually opted to come back in here. It's so bleak.'

'I think my tree brightens it a little bit,' I say, sweeping my hand out to the tangle of roots that leads up the hill to the silver-grey tree nodding in the wind. As I look at it, tiny buds begin to grow along the branches. Quickly they are blossoms, which curl and flutter down the hill, and then, as my magic swells, small pale globes appear.

'What are those?' Dylan whispers.

'Fruit!' I gasp, watching as they swell, white as snow. In moments they ripen, and break from the tree, rolling down towards us. I pick one up and hand it to Dylan. 'Try it!'

He grimaces. 'You made them with your mind!'

'So?'

'They might be a bit bitter,' he says, but his eyes are laughing, and when he takes a bite he doesn't immediately fall to the ground, poisoned. He just chews, for a long time, watching me.

I pick up another one, stroke my fingers against the downy, peach-like skin. 'Is it nice?'

'Try it,' he says, taking another bite.

I follow his lead, and my mouth is filled with the taste of golden honey and butter and sunshine and just a hint of spice, instantly warming me.

'Well, that's pretty good,' I say after a while, when we've both eaten down to the core. 'For an illusion, and all . . .'

'It's amazing,' Dylan says, putting another one in his pocket.

'You try it,' I whisper.

'What?'

'Io always said you could have changed this place. You should try, before we leave.'

He squints at me. 'Do what to it, though? Flood it with water?'

'I don't know – it's your magic, not mine!'

He huffs and looks around, kicking at the snow. When it flurries up from his foot, it is no longer snow, but tiny threads of ice. He frowns, and keeps kicking at snow, lifting his arms, his eyes shining. The threads gather, and he sweeps up more and more, until I'm standing on the only patch of snow, and rising up from the pale, grass-covered ground is a great ice sculpture, a huge monument to the great shaggy golden dog that is Helios, dwarfing my tiny, slender tree.

'Wow,' is all I can manage, when Dylan turns to me. Helios's frozen eyes gleam in the sun, and I feel a sharp pang at the thought of him being lost here somewhere.

'Look what I did!' he says, sounding as tired as I feel.

'Look what you did!'

He gazes around, taking a great, deep breath, and then marches over to the glass at the edge. 'We have to get out of here and find the real thing!'

'We do!' I say. 'To the fox world!'

He grins, and we rush around the edges of the globe, looking for the autumn tree with its pile of fallen leaves, but the fox world isn't there any more. Instead we find scrubby moorland with an iron-grey tower that has bars at every window, a solitary figure standing at the top, surveying the dismal sky. On the other side is another field, this one wild with heather and grasses, a golden dawn making everything glow.

'She must have re-ordered them.' Dylan frowns, peering in through the glass.

'Io? Or Ganymede?'

He shrugs. 'Either. Both. They had a deal – Ganymede would control the outside, and Io would control the inside – and they left each other to it . . .'

'They're as bad as each other,' I say. 'Let's try this way.'

Dylan nods, and we pull ourselves through the warp in the glass to the dawn. Seedheads nod all around us, and the air is thick with wishes. The grass reaches up to our waists, and crickets *chirr* deep within. The sky is a sweep of pale gold, turning to pink on the horizon. We spread our arms and run our fingers over the tips of the dry stalks, treading carefully as we start to search for the way out. It's warm here, though, and after all the chaos of Ganymede's house it's hard to rush.

'What does it feel like?' Dylan asks. 'Knowing you might see her soon, after all this time?'

'I don't know,' I say. 'I'm trying not to think about it too much. I don't really know what happened; if she's here, why she's stayed so long . . .'

'Time passes strangely,' he says. 'Maybe she doesn't know it's been years.'

'Is that better or worse, though?' I ask, catching at wishes and releasing them, unused.

'It would mean she didn't leave you on purpose.'

'Which is a good thing. But . . . I don't even know if I'd recognize her, Dylan. I don't know her at all. She missed so much.'

'Yeah.'

'Thank you for saying what you did to Ganymede.'

He shrugs, his sadness filling the air between us. He doesn't say it, but it's there. His dad *isn't* here. However far we travel, however many worlds we find, he won't be here.

'What was he like?'

'Tall,' he says after a long silence as we reach the middle of the field. Glass winks in the distance, and somewhere over there is another globe. 'He had a beard, so he was always scratchy. He was away a lot with work, but when he came back he'd bring something from wherever he'd been. Nothing special: just driftwood, or pebbles, shells. Once an old coin.' He blows at the wishes that drift too close. 'He laughed a lot. And he was messy. Mum used to despair.'

'He sounds a bit like a pirate,' I say.

'That's what she called him when she was cross.' He smiles. 'Ole piratehead.'

We keep walking towards the other side of the glass,

the dry grass rustling as we go, heat broken by a gentle summer breeze.

'So I reckon we look for Io's globe,' I say. 'I think we'll feel her magic when we get closer; it was so strong before. And then we'll just have to deal with her and get her to hand over Helios and my mum. What do you think?'

'I guess it's as good a plan as any.' Dylan sighs. 'It would be nice if we found them without having to deal with her.'

'We can hope,' I say, and then there's a roll of thunder that makes the earth quake beneath our feet. 'What was that?'

'A storm?'

'Doesn't feel like . . .'

The thunder gets louder, the ground trembles and a great white stallion comes flying towards us, steam rising from its flanks, its rider shouting, 'Yah! Yah!' We throw ourselves out of the way as the horse comes to a sudden stop, shying and snorting, the rider falling with a crash of metal to the ground.

'Godforsaken steed,' comes a dark mutter.

Dylan and I pick ourselves up, and the pile of metal slowly unfolds, rising with a clatter and a creak to form the shape of a man in armour, helmet slightly squashed over his head. He pulls it off with a curse and stares at us.

'So here you are,' he says, turning in a circle round us, his nose in the air. He is quite short. His curly brown hair is stuck to his head with sweat, and he sounds like a clash of pans when he moves. 'I have heard of you – ruinous children, come to thwart our lady.'

I sigh.

'Ah, 'tis not so bad,' says the man. 'For I have heard tale that you offer freedom! Is that right?' He stalks towards his mighty horse and with a command the great white animal drops to its knees so that the little man can climb back up. 'Is it?' he demands, looking down on us.

'That's our plan,' I say, but it comes out a little bit choked because his beautiful horse is not a horse at all. There's a great shining horn at the centre of its forehead. 'Is that . . . is it a unicorn?' I step closer as the unicorn scrambles to its feet, and cautiously lay my hand against its neck. I feel coarse hair, the beat of its heart, the sweep of eyelashes as it looks down at me and blinks huge dark eyes.

'Why yes!' says the man, pulling nervously at the

reins when the unicorn lowers its head to sniff at me.

I stroke its nose, trying to breathe in the whole sense of it. A unicorn! After all those daydreams, all those imagined adventures, I'm actually stroking a unicorn!

'But not really,' says Dylan.

'What do you mean, young sir?' demands the man.

'You're a magician, so you've made your horse look like a unicorn, haven't you?'

I give Dylan a withering look as the unicorn pulls away from me.

'It's probably a little donkey in real life,' Dylan says, skirting the animal.

The man gives a gasp and starts to rummage at his belt.

'Dylan!'

'Sorry,' he says. 'I'm very sorry, sir.'

He gives a little bow, and the man looks appeased, though I can still see the twinkle in Dylan's eye.

'I am Sir Jones,' says the man. 'And this is my gallant steed, Eugene –' the steed whinnies, as if in agreement– 'who is most certainly not a small donkey, not in any reality we might consider.' He pulls his helmet back on.

'I came to let you know that we cannot help you. By all that is right, we should hold you here and alert our lady. However, we are tired. We spent the night at a party two globes over. We will take our leave, and imagine ourselves to have dreamed of two little children with mischief on their minds. And when we wake we will know that even in our dreams we did not help them, did not guide them on the *right path*.' He winks and points over to our left, leaning down. 'But go *quick*, for my lady is on the *warpath* and looking just for you!'

He yanks on Eugene's reins and gallops off with a clatter, a cloud of wishes following in his wake.

'Think we can trust him?' Dylan asks, looking in the direction Sir Jones pointed.

'Yes,' I say. 'I think we can. If he has the heart to imagine himself a unicorn, I'm sure he has the heart to imagine freedom.' And I strop off without him in a rustle of grass.

The next world is a tiny town, perched near the top of a mountain, only its crown caught in the globe. We should be cold – every narrow winding street glitters with frost, and twisted spindles of ice line the eaves of the rounded, scrunched-together houses. Candles are lit in the windows, and somewhere in the distance children are singing. Trees line the streets, and there are tiny lights set in all the branches. Overhead, stars wink between shifting clouds, which dust the little thatched roofs in snow as they pass.

'This kind of winter isn't so bad,' Dylan says, his eyes glowing as we edge past the clock tower that perches in the middle of the town, trying not to alert the magician here to our presence.

I can feel their magic, tinsel-bright and warm, but ahead is the pull of Io's own power, making the stone in my ring glow bright as a small red sun, and I don't want to be diverted now. I don't want her to find us before we find her.

'This way,' I say, crunching up over a little bridge to where the glass sweeps down, a pucker in its surface clearly visible.

'But I can smell gingerbread,' Dylan complains, his eyes lingering on the clock tower, where the magician's presence is strongest. 'Maybe the kind of person who has gingerbread would know where Helios is . . . He might have been drawn here!'

'When was gingerbread ever a good thing?' I whisper, pulling him onward. 'Gingerbread houses mean children in ovens, Dylan – all the stories say so. Let's hope Helios *didn't* get drawn here!'

'We make a gingerbread house every year,' he protests. 'And we don't bake children – or dogs!'

'You are not a magician in a snowglobe.'

He grins. 'Actually I am. So are you!'

I reach out with a laugh, put my hand through the ripple . . . and we're sucked into the next world, where it feels as if Io is already in full storm. The night sky is dense, and the ground is a plunging, swooping carpet of glittering midnight-blue sand. A solitary winter tree is the only feature, and we scrabble over to it, clinging to its thick, rough trunk as everything shakes. Something calls from overhead, and when we look up there's a shadow clinging to one of the branches, only its eyes clearly visible, glinting at us.

My lady! calls the shadow in a thin voice. *They are here! If you would only stop your tumult, you would see . . . they are here!*

But the storm continues, the sand shifting beneath us, the whole world swooping up and over, tiny golden stars spinning down from the sky, their edges cutting into our skin. For a split second I can see a huge eye staring in at us, but Dylan loses his grip on the tree, and I dive for him, clutching at his shirt as we're turned head over heels, over and over, until we crash against the glass edge of the world and straight through, into cold, clear water.

25

My breath escapes in tiny bubbles, and I don't know which way is up. Dylan swims over to me while I flounder, losing feeling in my limbs, and propels us to the surface. A low, flat wooden jetty rises up on stilts beside us – we're in a lake, a wooden cabin on the grassy shore, cherry blossom trees shedding their petals all around it. Dylan pushes me out of the water and I flop on to the jetty, spluttering and shivering.

'Ganymede,' I manage finally, my throat hoarse, when he's dragged himself up after me, lying face up, breathing hard.

'What?'

'The storm wasn't Io – it was Ganymede. I saw her looking in. She's searching, Dylan, shaking up all the worlds to find us.'

'That's all we need,' he whispers. 'Both of them turning everything upside down. What was that thing in the last place?' He shudders. 'Made my skin prickle.'

'Definitely someone on Io's side,' I say, flipping on to my back and staring up at the sky. Somewhere here is a magician, so we should be leaping up and moving on, but I'm so tired.

'Or some*thing*,' Dylan says.

'They're all people, though, aren't they? All the magicians. Just people with magic, like us.'

'I'm not like that!'

'Maybe you would be if you'd been in here for a couple of hundred years.'

'Are we going to let them all out when this is over? Even the bad ones?'

I sit up, crossing my legs and looking at the wood cabin at the other end of the jetty. 'I guess so. I mean, people are all sorts, aren't they? Can't lock them all away just because they give us the creeps.'

'If they do something bad, though . . .'

'Then it would be human-bad, with added magic. They'd end up in prison.'

He frowns and drags himself over to sit by me.

'I don't know. Not if they could make themselves invisible. Or fly, or something.'

'I've not seen anyone here with that kind of power. My mum's book says power is just an extension of nature. Like you, with water. And she says Ganymede is all about silver and the moon. And Io is gold and the sun and stormy passion, which we've seen plenty of already.'

'What's your mum?'

'Earth. Gardening.' I sigh. 'Which is what I seem to have inherited.'

'What's wrong with that? I liked your flowers, back at school.'

'I just never pictured myself as a gardener. I mean, I enjoyed fixing her garden a bit, but I'm not sure it's really me.'

'Maybe we haven't worked you out yet,' Dylan says, getting slowly to his feet and holding his hand out. 'You could be a bit of all of it. Look what happened with Jago . . .'

'I think that would happen to anyone if they had magic and didn't know how to use it,' I say, letting him pull me up.

'Here, let me try something,' he says, frowning at my

shivers. 'Maybe I could . . .' He narrows his eyes, makes a flicking motion with his hands, and droplets of water fly away from me, spattering on to the jetty. 'Oof,' he mutters, turning a bit pale. 'That was quite a lot.'

'You did it!' I grin, looking down at my dry clothes, reaching up to touch my dry hair. 'That's amazing! Can you do it for yourself?'

He mumbles a bit and draws his hands together over his chest before sweeping them out in the same motion. Water flies up into the sun, making tiny rainbows. I dart out of the way before I get drenched again, and he falls to his knees on the jetty, dry but completely exhausted.

'Need a bit of practice,' he says with a pale smile, as a young woman bursts out of the cabin and runs on to the jetty. She's more like a fairy than a person: light and nimble, her dark hair caught up high in a tight bun, white dress floating around her knees.

'Oh but, dears – you mustn't force your magic that way; you'll hurt yourselves!' she cries in a soft voice, sweeping over to us, her brown feet silent on the wood. 'My, but look at you both: you're so new and shiny! How on earth did you end up here? Was it Io? Has she transplanted you here to keep an eye on me?' She draws back with a frown. 'But no. You are not spies. You are more like hunters! What are you hunting, my dears? May I help?'

She seems to question herself, dancing to the edge of the jetty and looking down into the water as if it might have the answers. 'I may!' She laughs, turning back to us. 'I am myself, and myself approves of this. So tell me, dears, what is it you seek? Let me guess, let me guess – I am sure I can . . .'

She steps around us, her dark eyes glittering, blossoms sweeping from the trees that surround her cabin. 'Both here for heart, I see, so much the better. You –' she stares up at Dylan, her face turning serious – 'for your dear puppy; the one who saw you through so much misery.' She reaches up and flicks him on one ear, earning a surprised yelp from him. 'You must not dwell in that misery much longer, dear soul. Your father is still within; he will *never* leave you. And you have magic! And heart! You have much!' She nods, as if satisfied.

'Now you . . .' She turns to me, putting her head on one side like a little curious bird. 'You. For your ma, who left you so long ago. Oh, she didn't mean to! It is writ in you, bold as blood. She is here, you know.' Her mouth twists. 'Io has your answers. Oh, dear. You must face Io.'

She backs away from us. 'Now let me see, let me see if I can help. Ah! Yes!'

She puts two fingers in her mouth, leans forward, her eyes intent upon the cherry blossoms, and lets forth a piercing whistle. It resounds through the snowglobe, makes ripples in the lake, sends whole branches of blossom cascading into the air. And then, through the trees, a familiar shape comes bounding, golden fur catching the light, tongue lolling from a huge doggy smile.

'Helios!' Dylan cries, running to meet him.

I watch, not breathing, as they pelt towards each other and meet in a crash of bodies. Helios jumps up and puts his paws on Dylan's shoulders, his head resting into his neck, as Dylan puts his arms round his furry body, and they stand like that for the longest moment, while our new friend dances on her tiptoes with delight, and I try to keep my tears silent.

'Oh, my dear, let them fall!' she says, turning to see me. 'It is a help, is it not? I cannot fix the rest for you, and there is far to go. At least now you do it with your faithful friend. At least now you may search for just one, yes?'

'Yes. Thank you,' I say, grinning as Dylan turns to me, and Helios comes flying over, knocking me back on to the jetty and covering me with slobber.

'How did you do that?' Dylan asks the magician, once the commotion has died away a little and we're sitting on the edge of the jetty, Helios lying between us. 'Who are you?'

'Fabia,' she says, tucking her hands beneath her legs, her feet swishing in the water. 'Should you need a label. I don't wear them well. It wasn't so hard to reunite you; he's been searching for you.' She smiles. 'He doesn't like the one he came in with; he's not the kindest. It was the least I could do . . . the rest is up to you. You are on the right track,' she assures us, her dark eyes sober. 'And your ring will be a guide, my dear. But there is far to go, through the forest and the fortress itself. Io keeps her deepest secrets in there; I am sure you will find what you need once you get inside. Use your magic – you will need it – and remember that, while there are tricksters in here, there are many of us who are with you, in spirit if not body.'

'Why are there so many who are happy to stay? They seem to love Io!' I say.

'Some of us had a difficult time in that real world of yours,' she says. 'For some, it was easier to be in here, easier to hide, to play with magic unencumbered by rules or consequences. Io is very good at that! For others, it was lonely. All of this –' she spreads her arms – 'it is beautiful, yes? And my mind believes in it, ninety-nine per cent. But that one per cent . . .' She sighs. 'That one per cent is lonely here, with only illusion for company. And I never did get the smell of the cherry blossoms quite right. I will be glad to be back in my rightful place, my dear, and even those who have become spoilt here will be fine once they are home again. They will learn to be, and that is right. We who have magic must also have some control of it! So, my dears, have faith. Bring the whole house down!' Her voice rumbles slightly as she says it – as if she speaks for many – and the blossoms whirl faster, wilder, until she jumps up with alarm.

'But quick!' she says. 'Io is on the prowl. She has left the way clear! Flee, my warriors, into the lair, through the black ice that her magic has become, and the mists of her illusions, and into the heart of the sun!'

She stamps her foot, the world shudders, and we're already running to the glass wall, to the place where it swims. Helios jumps around us, and her words echo in my ears as we push ourselves through.

26

Three moons glow in a twilight sky, making an arc over the tangled forest that fills this new world. The largest is all swirls of silver and grey; the middle one darker, shot with bursts of amber light; and the smallest is yellow-gold, pitted and streaked with shadows.

'Stick to the glass,' Dylan hisses behind me. 'If we just follow it round . . .'

But something is calling to me, with a song that catches me inside and makes the red stone in my ring gleam bright. My feet move of their own accord to the edge of the trees, and Dylan is saying something, his voice rising in protest, but I don't stop. I keep going, though my skin is all static and goosebumps.

The branches writhe, and shadows creep. The whole place twists and tangles, and the pale wood is weeping.

I try not to touch anything. It feels like a trap, like a spider's web.

'Clem!' Dylan's voice is thin. It comes from a million miles away.

I force myself to turn away from the song's call and back to him. He's forcing his way through a snarl of dense undergrowth, Helios stepping gingerly behind him. I don't remember coming through it and, as I watch, it thickens between us, trees leaning in, creaking as their branches spread above his head.

'What's going on?' he shouts, wincing as spools of thorn-covered vines whip over the hard, moss-covered ground.

It's my mother's song and it pulls at me, but we're being separated, and I can't let that happen. The brambles settle as I get closer, and I stretch out to help him over the twining branches. A howl shudders through the woods as the thorns lose their grip on him, and Helios ruffs as he scrambles over to join us, pricking his ears. Shadows twist through the branches, and creatures scuttle, their glowing eyes blinking at us from high overhead and in the deep, dark undergrowth.

'What was that?' Dylan asks, his breath steaming.

'A wolf?' I shudder. 'I don't know. We should keep going.'

We stand back to back, turning, searching for a clear path. I twist the ring on my finger absently as the lilt of the song flutters at me, drawing me in, and the stone lights up with a glow that makes my whole hand a torch.

'Where do we go?' Dylan asks, staring at the light.

I point to the middle of the forest, where the trees get darker, and the strange shifting light of the moons cuts through the scattering clouds. Just visible over the treetops is a slice of darkness – a black tower that rings with a song only I can hear.

'There,' I say. 'That's Io's lair. That's where my mother is.'

He looks from me to the tower, his fingers deep in Helios's curling golden coat. 'Are you sure?'

'I can hear her,' I say. 'Her song.'

'It could be Io,' he says. 'Calling you, trying to trick you and trap you.'

'It's a risk.' I bite my lip. 'You don't have to come, but this is the right way, Dylan. Fabia said something about Io's lair being the black ice of her magic, and there we'd find the heart . . .' I try to remember the order, through the constant pull of the song. 'I'm sure Ganymede called my mother her "dearest heart".'

He nods, and I can see that he's not convinced, but he doesn't back away. He stands by my side, looking at the tower.

'I can feel her, Dylan.'

'OK,' he says. 'Let's do it. We're not defenceless.'

'No, we have our guard dog.' I smile, as Helios tucks himself behind Dylan.

'And we have magic,' Dylan says. His eyes shine in the flicker of the ring's light.

I feed the ring with everything I have inside me until it's a small sun, and we stagger along, half dazzled by its light, through the trees that snarl and wither away from us. They thin gradually until we're out on a broad plain where a black river rushes and strange night-glowing flowers fill the air with a heavy scent. From here the tower is a glittering black house, a twisted gothic palace with balconies, tiny bridges, gargoyles and grotesques climbing every wall, and great sweeping steps that lead up to a huge porch with carved pillars. Spires stretch to the sky, sharpening to needle-points. It is a negative image of Ganymede's house: the absolute inverse of that gleaming white shard. Io has made her own, with all her magic, and it is so dark it's hard even to look at it for long.

Overhead, the three moons are bright and full as lanterns. My ring's bright glow softens as I tread forward, but as I get closer I can feel something else. Something dark and powerful that reaches out and searches the night, hungry for blood. Something that twists through my mother's song and makes my head swim.

I brace myself to face whatever might be in there, but Dylan shouts behind me, and I spin round just as a lone wolf breaks free of the forest, silver fur standing up on edge along its spine, teeth bared, launching itself straight at Helios, who has rushed forward with a frenzied bark.

'No!' Dylan shouts as the two skirt each other.

The wolf is just as enormous as Helios, but there's a ferocity in its mirror eyes that I've never seen in our dog. It darts and snaps at Helios, who growls, lowering himself, preparing to leap at the wolf.

Dylan spreads his arms wide and looks up to the sky, and the strands of cloud that spool around the moons begin to gather, getting thicker, swelling with rain.

With the flick of a hand, he bursts the clouds, and rain pours down around us, fat drops that splash against the hard ground, turning it into a shallow pool beneath our feet. The wolf backs away from Helios, staring up at Dylan with a deep, throaty growl, and launches itself at him.

'STOP!' I shout.

The stone in the ring dazzles, and everything stops: the wolf in mid-air, Helios rushing up towards it, and Dylan leaning away. The trees, the song, the rain – everything stops. I take a breath, standing beneath three strange moons in a frozen world, and the effort of the magic swells inside my head until I can't stand it any more. I shove Dylan, as hard as I can, just to buy us a moment. He crashes to the ground and slides through wet mud, away from the wolf, and then I let the pressure go. The song rushes back in, the dark strand still running through it, and the wolf falls slavering to the ground, its target now metres away.

Dylan scrambles up, shivering and covered in mud, Helios rushing to him, and I stand over the wolf, steeling myself, just hoping I've worked it out right. When it rises to its full height, I look it square in the eye.

'*Go home*,' I say, and the ring glows, my magic a new song that washes through the world. The sky prickles with stars, the moons pulse and the trees draw back. The wolf stares at me for a long moment, and then turns tail, heading into the forest.

'How did you do that?' Dylan demands, slithering over the mud to me.

'Magic.' I smile, my heart thudding in my ears, fingertips numb from the shock of it all.

'But how did you know it would work?'

'It's Io's wolf,' I say. 'I saw how it reacted to your magic, and I'm Io's family, so I figured it would recognize me if I used my magic. At least, that it would follow an order . . .'

'That was a big risk,' he says, frowning and looking from me to the black house that looms over us. 'What if it hadn't?'

'Then I'd be wolf pie, and you'd be here alone with Helios. So it's a good job I was right.'

He stares at me. 'You are not who I thought you were.'

'Neither are you.'

'I mean, when we were at school, before all this . . . sometimes it was like you weren't there at all. Like you were sleepwalking. And now we're here, where I feel like I'm dreaming most of the time, and you're stomping through it all like you're a queen!'

I frown at him. I never thought of it as sleepwalking, but it's true that I wasn't always in the real world. All the missed rounders balls, all the times I was glared at for staring, that's what was happening: thinking, watching, imagining.

'I'm not saying it's a bad thing,' he says.

'It's easier here,' I say, turning to look back at the house. 'Easy to see where there's danger, or to tell if someone is on your side. At school, people are more complicated.'

27

There's a war going on in my blood. My mother's song is calling so sweetly, filling me up and making my footsteps sure as we head towards the tower. But winding round it like the brambles in my mother's garden is that other tune, a thread of fear, with everything we've already seen, and what we might still face. My own doubt, snaring me.

'OK?' asks Dylan as I hesitate.

The dark tower looms over us, and the whole place seems to reverberate with power.

'Yes.' I clench my fists at my sides and put my foot on the first step. Ice flashes through me and I bite my lip, whispering a warning to Dylan, who flinches and turns pale as he joins me. 'Are you sure you want to come with me?'

'*Want* isn't quite the word,' he whispers. 'But yes. I'm coming.'

Helios, however, isn't budging. He sits on the scrubby ground just in front of the steps and won't move, no matter how hard we cajole.

'We can't leave him again,' Dylan says. 'What do we do?'

'We're not leaving him,' I say. 'We're trusting him to watch our backs. '

Dylan gives me a withering look, and I shrug.

'What can we do? Stay with him, Dylan, if that feels right. I'll be fine.'

I turn my back on both of them before I can change my mind and make my way further up the staircase. Every footstep is like the strike of a bell, and every step takes at least three paces. Three strikes, three flashes of ice threading through me. I keep my eyes on the massive porch at the top. One step away, and there's a trap. I remember Ganymede talking about traps and wards when I first went into her house. It didn't feel those, though. These traps, they're like teeth.

Lightning strikes, spidering in veins down the entire building, bursting into fire all around me. I close my eyes and breathe deeply, forcing it away as my mother's

239

song swells, and when I look up the last flickers of the lightning are spiriting away across the black stone. My skin is warm, and Dylan is by my side, breathless, his hair standing on end.

'What happened?' I ask.

'You lit up!' he says. 'I ran to pull you out of the way. You were just standing there with your eyes closed, and you just –' he spreads his hands – 'lit up like a torch!'

'It was her,' I say, my eyes filling up. 'My mother's song, Dylan. I could feel it inside me.'

'It was you,' he says.

'What about Helios?'

'I trust him,' he says. His voice is a bit wobbly, but there's grit in it that was never there before, and we open the huge front door together.

She is here. She has to be here.

28

The floor inside is an ice rink. I try to keep my footsteps soft and small as we dart through the vast, echoing hallway, because Io will be on her way. She will have felt the strike of lightning, she will be here any moment, and the knowledge is like wire in my chest.

'This place is a nightmare,' whispers Dylan, his eyes wide as we head up the stairs, our hands on the shining banister.

There are paintings everywhere of night skies and rose-gold dawns breaking over wild seas. Of wild horses, and tumbledown castles. Mist starts to gather around our feet.

'Are you sure your mother is here, Clem?'

I swallow hard and nod, hoping, *willing* it to be true.

Up on the next floor, there's a full-blown fog,

clinging to the walls and whispering along the ceiling. The pictures light up as we pass, like windows into strange, alien worlds of shadowy landscapes and blue moons, and tiny figures in the distance, beckoning us in.

'This is not good,' Dylan says with a shudder. 'She can see us, Clem. All these paintings are like eyes – she knows exactly where we are!'

His eyes are wild, and I remember when I first found him, how terrified he was of her. How cruel she could be.

'She won't win. Not now. Not between your magic and mine.'

'How can you be so sure?'

'I'm not saying it's going to be easy,' I say. 'But don't you feel it, Dylan? There's so much power here, and it's not all on her side. Three moons in the sky, three sisters, and now you and me. She's only one person, Dylan, no matter how magical.'

Clementine. The song is stronger, wilder, now. She's here; I'm so sure of it. I stalk onward, through winding corridors where the paintings show scenes of three young sisters, weaving on looms, reading by candlelight.

'*Clementine*,' Dylan whispers, his brown eyes flashing.

A blast of light behind us bleaches out everything, just for an instant. *'She's here!'*

'Clever things, aren't you?' Io says, butterflies spinning up into the air as we turn to see her come. Her voice is a heavy gold bell ringing out against the fog, cutting through everything.

'What did you do?' I whisper.

'What do you mean, my dear? Why are you here? It's brave, I'll grant you, but perhaps a little foolish, to venture straight into the heart of it all.'

'Where is she?' I ask. 'What have you done with her, Io? Why have you kept her here so long?'

It bursts out in a torrent that rolls through the corridor, sending sparks flying, cracks running up the walls.

Dylan stares at me, but I can see the blue spark of magic in his eyes, and I know he is fighting hard just not to get caught in her web. I'm on my own here. I should have kept running. I should have kept my mouth shut.

'Clementine,' she says, a smile on her mouth. 'So it is true. You are kin!' She clasps her hands together. Her hazel eyes are warm and full of joy. 'Our dearest really had a *daughter*, and now you are here! You are come!'

'I am come to get her,' I hiss. 'And take her away from you!'

'Oh, you are like her,' she says, smiling wider. 'I knew it! I wondered the first time I saw you, and then Ganymede was fluttering about in a panic talking of babies long-grown, and now you are here, and just as heartful as your mother, and your rage is like fire!' She pauses. 'But I cannot let you go, my dearest. Nor your mother. You are both too bright. Ganymede may not have you. You belong here with me!'

She reaches out, the butterflies beating in the air around us, and I thrust out my hand too hard, too sure. '*Stop!*'

And everything does. Io is a statue, her hazel eyes watching intently even as the rest of her can do nothing. Dylan is frozen, caught by her side. Particles that shone in the bright of a thousand golden candles are static in the air, the flames unflickering.

I stopped it all.

'Good,' I say, and before the spell is broken I run up the narrow staircase to the tower room that I know will be there, round and round, all the time caught in the singing web of my mother's voice, until it opens up before me. The moons shine through a glass domed ceiling, and in the centre, surrounded by pictures of forests and bright, sparkling cities, is a single gleaming brass pedestal, a single snowglobe, glowing like a small sun.

Within the globe is another house, this one built of old stone, ramshackle and dilapidated, but vibrant with colour. Every window is alight; every balcony a riot of flowers. The gardens teem with life, small birds spiral from place to place, and on the top step, between two blooming trees, sits a woman. She is smiling as she sings her sad song. She doesn't look up. She doesn't notice me at all.

Now she's in front of me, and I can see her breath on the glass. After a lifetime of imagining, I could almost reach out and touch her, but she's more lost to me than ever. Why did I imagine she'd been stolen from me in some fairytale disaster? She isn't missing me. She's a dream caught in glass. My dream.

She has dark hair and dark eyes, and her dress is green, and her song is breaking me apart. I don't know how to break Io's spell.

How do I break this thing? I demand.

She looks up. Her eyes widen.

Who are you?

I cannot answer – my heart is stuck in my throat.

WHO ARE YOU?

She looks straight at me, her hands twisted together.

I stare at her, take in every inch of her. That is my mother. Not a warrior queen who stalked by my side into school, not a tragic princess locked away by wicked witches. Not any of the images I'd fed myself over the years. She is a woman. A real blood-and-bone woman, small and full of complicated things. I hold her in my heart, just the way she is. I see the way her hair curls as it escapes its bun, the dry flowers that still nestle there, the chapped skin on her hands, the shine of her shadowed eyes as she looks at me.

'*Come out*,' I shout then, raising my hands, my voice resonating with all the dreams and fantasies that were never really her, as I send it all out. My breath is hot. It curls like steam in the air, and static rolls over the glass. Petals fly inside the globe, bricks crack and the house begins to collapse behind her. I pull harder and the glass warps, shattering and sending a million shards out into the room. I close my eyes against their sting, and when I open them again there she is, standing before me, in a muddle of the things that kept her there all those years.

She is static, still caught in my spell, but tears well up in her eyes as she stares at me.

She is crying.

I am angry. I am made of towering rock, glinting and bright, and she is crying.

'I needed you.'

Clementine? No, but I am dreaming. This cannot be! IO! Break this spell. Let me move!

'It isn't Io's spell,' I whisper. 'Io's spell shut you in the globe. This is mine, and it's keeping everything still for a moment so I can think!'

Let me go! she bursts. *Please, I do not understand – break this spell!*

Make everything go again? Wake Io and her cursed butterflies, the candles and the war in my blood? I'm afraid that if I let go, it's going to be too big, and the whole house will fall apart.

I can't.

You can.

Her eyes are intent. She smells of the earth and the stars, a deep, metallic scent that washes over me and takes me to a memory of sunshine and a bright, light kitchen, the windows open to the garden, and my ma, singing, happy.

How has she been here all this time, content in her make-believe, while I grew up?

Clementine!

Nobody else ever said it like that; even if they had tried, they never could have made it ring. The spell I cast to trap Io has become a thick knot in my mind and it grows, the longer I hold on to it, until my head is pounding. I reach out and touch the sleeve of her dress, and it's real. The flowers in her hair begin to bloom.

She is real.

My spell breaks, the knot unwinds with a snap that makes my ears ring and noise ricochets around me: Io's screech, the thunder of a storm outside and cracks that spread up the walls to the ceiling with a terrible ripping sound. The candles stutter into life once more.

'Clementine?' my mother whispers, rushing to me, holding my arms tight, her dark eyes looking deep into mine, flitting to take in every part of me. 'Is it you?'

I nod.

'But you are all grown up,' she says. 'How can this be? I saw you this morning. I left you with your pa, and you were tiny – a whirl of joy and temper. You are only two . . . you cannot be this! What happened? What did they do?'

The cracks in the ceiling widen as my heart stutters. She doesn't have the answers, she only has questions, and I don't know what to do with all the shock and grief spilling out of her.

'How old are you, Clementine?'

'Twelve.'

The tears fall. The glass dome shatters, and the moons over our heads are brighter than ever.

'How did this *happen*?' she whispers, looking up, and then back to me. 'Where are my sisters? What did they do? How can this . . . ? Oh, Clementine, my sweet girl, I have missed so much. Oh *Piotr* . . .' She lets go of me, puts her hands to her mouth. 'Your dear pa. Such a little row . . . have I really left you both for so long! Where is he now?'

'He's at home,' I say. 'He . . . didn't know where you went. He gave me your book, and I found the house, and Ganymede was there. She says she put you in here because she thought you weren't happy . . .' My own tears start to fall. 'She didn't know you had me – you didn't *tell* them – so she put you in a globe so you could be with Io and she could comfort you. And then Io hid you here.'

'It was a day!' she says. 'I thought it was just a day.

That is Io's magic; I didn't feel it! What have they done to us, Clementine? We were happy. We were a family!' She brushes the tears from her cheeks and takes a breath. 'We will fix it.'

'What do you mean?'

'We can use magic.' Her eyes dance with sudden possibility. 'We can . . . we can make it so that your memories are mine, so that it has been but a day. Your pa, as well. We will all be together, in here. And time will mean nothing.'

'You can't turn back time! You can't make me two again! You can't take back everything that happened while you were in here – that's my life! Pa's life!'

'You have lived it all without me,' she whispers after a long silence. 'So then what do we do?'

'We go home,' I say.

'We go home,' she repeats. 'But don't you hate me, for having left you for so long?'

I can't answer that, not right now.

She looks at me long and hard, and then nods, a decision made. She takes my hand in hers, kisses me hard on the forehead and then lifts her face to the dome above us.

'IO!' she roars.

The windows in the tower break, the glass blows out and the whole house rings like a bell with her fury. She storms out of the tower room, pulling me along behind her, and her footsteps are like thunder as we go.

29

The house is falling down around us. With every step it shudders, rolling like a ship at sea. The cracks have splintered every wall, and the paintings hang lop-sided, some of them crashing to the floor. My mother's hand is small but strong, her stride unrelenting as she sweeps through the corridors, her skirts like a forest, the flowers in her hair blooming brighter all the time.

'IO!' she shouts again, bursting into the main passageway, pulling us down the stairs. 'Where are you? Stop hiding from me!'

There's movement in the hallway below, and Io flashes past us, running for the vast front door, Dylan close behind her. We race down steps that crack beneath our feet as the trees in the forest begin to fall with a groan.

'What are you doing?' Io demands as we emerge

at the front of the house. Her hair is a haystack, her copper cloak unravelling at the bottom. 'Callisto! Calm yourself!'

Dylan edges past her and rushes over to me with Helios as I pull myself away from my mother.

'What did you do?' he asks. 'Everything went dark, and then Io was racing for the tower – I tried to stop her, and then she heard your ma shout, and the whole place started to fall down! I've never seen Io frightened before!'

'I just got her out,' I whisper. 'That's all.'

I can't stop staring at them. They're like wild animals stalking each other, and the fury in the air between them is so fierce it threatens to turn us all into embers. We draw back as the tower behind us lurches with a great screech, falling through the floors of the house, dust and chips of black stone flying out all around us. The bridge cracks and breaks in two, and the three of us race across the scrubby ground to stand by the black river, watching as the sisters face each other in the rubble, barely flinching in the chaos.

'Calm myself? Look what you've done!' my mother yells, throwing out a hand in my direction, clouds rumbling overhead, obscuring the three moons the sisters were named for.

Io had everything here, I realize, looking up. Her sisters in the sky with her, and all the paintings of all the worlds they'd made inside the house. She made a world within a world, and she missed nothing.

'You with your warped magic – look how it has darkened while you've locked yourself in here! All of this illusion doesn't change anything, Io. You have used this place as your own private entertainment, and you trapped me here because you could not bear to let me free, and I have missed everything! I have missed my daughter growing up!'

'I didn't know you had a daughter!' Io flings back at her, golden skirts flying as she's forced back from the ruin of her house, her sister darting in the other direction in a whirl of green. 'Had you trusted us, we would have known! We would never have taken you away from your only child. Why didn't you tell us, Callisto?'

'I was afraid! I knew Gan would say she had magic and must be controlled, and I couldn't bear that. I was so *tired* of you both, all the arguments and the power struggles – and now look what you've done! You have taken my heart and I can never get it back, Io . . . There are ten years of her childhood that I will never know! How can I go home after all this time? How can I make it right? I loved them more than the earth and stars, Io – more than anything!' She stamps her foot and tears at her chest and yells with such force that the ground beneath us shudders. 'You have ruined me!'

'I have not!' Io replies with a catch in her voice. 'I have not, Callisto. They are still there. They will love you still. How could they not? I am sorry! I am so sorry . . .'

Her voice breaks, and the clouds overhead crash together. Great fat drops of rain begin to fall around us. The river beside us rises in a tide, and the sky darkens ominously.

'Are you doing that?' I whisper to Dylan.

'I don't know,' he says.

'They haven't even noticed,' I say as the river breaks its banks and starts to flood over the dry ground.

My mother and Io are still circling each other; they don't hear us calling. They don't see the water rising. They can only see each other's desperation, and I can barely see anything because my eyes won't stop making tears. She's here, and she is just what Pa said she was.

She's a force of nature, and I can only stand and watch.

'We have to go!' Dylan shouts. 'The storm is getting worse – it's not safe!'

'We can't just leave them!' I protest as the two sisters move closer together, their breath misting in the air, sparks still flying even as rain pounds down around us. The river has reached our ankles already and the house is a great mound of rubble.

'We can,' he says, grabbing my hand and pulling me to the glass wall that curves from the river to the forest. 'You've done everything you can here. We'll get back to the house and break the globe, and they'll come back.' He doesn't wait. 'Let us IN!' he commands with a voice like flint, and the glass warps, and we are back in the house where all of this started.

It's ear-stretching quiet after all the chaos: just a narrow corridor, pale sunlight filtering through a narrow window, and the snowglobes on their shelves, all in a silent whirl. Io's globe stands before us, cracks already fracturing the glass. It seems impossible that Ganymede hasn't heard the racket, and yet it is all just within one tiny globe.

'Let's break it, then,' I whisper, once we've caught our breath.

'OK,' he says. 'Do you know how?'

'Don't you?' I ask. 'You seemed pretty sure when we were in there!'

'I wanted to get us out,' he says. 'And there was no way they were ever going to hear us.'

'Let's do it together,' I say. 'Our power combined . . . if we just blast it all at them, maybe the glass will shatter.'

We stand back a bit, and Helios retreats, sitting in the corner with a huff. Footsteps start to echo from far away: Ganymede will be here soon.

We need to do it now.

We hold hands, and focus on the globe. My mother and Io rush towards the glass on the other side, realizing we've already broken out, and then I hear Dylan's song for the first time. It's like the rush and tumble of a stream, like a waterfall, untamed and beautiful. I thread my song with his, gathering all my magic, everything I ever wanted or needed, and the waterfall flashes with gold, flowing from us to the snowglobe.

The glass breaks with a blast of magic that makes my hair stand on end, and the corridor fills with tiny particles of black dust.

And two women stand in the midst of it all, pale

with shock, staring at us, both of them drenched and breathless from all their shouting.

'Clementine!' my mother gasps. 'What did you do?'

'I got you out of there,' I say. 'With Dylan's help . . .'

She stares at us, but there is no more time for talk. The chandeliers flicker, the globes begin to swirl and Ganymede is upon us.

'What is this?' she demands, rushing along the corridor and stopping dead when she sees us all here, the candles in the sconces on the walls guttering. Her shock is so great that it's another wave of destruction, heading in our direction.

'Control yourself, sister,' says Io, rising up to her full height, running a shaking hand through her golden hair, butterflies spiralling out. 'Did you think we would be gone forever?'

Ganymede doesn't say anything. Her grey eyes are huge, shining like mirrors, looking between us all, lingering on my mother, who stands by my side, ashen-faced, her song a broken chord that flutters without end.

'I thought I'd lost you all,' Ganymede whispers. 'I thought I'd lost you, and it was my fault. I sent you all away.' Her song is a whispering thread of want and need and desperate, hiding loneliness. 'I thought I'd be alone forever,' she says. 'I was unkind, and it has always been the two of you against me, so you both went, and I was alone here. A hundred, a thousand years of solitude. What happened, Clementine? Is this your doing?'

'None of it is my doing!' I say. 'The three of you did it all!'

'And you brought them back here, after all this time,' she says.

'It was ten years,' I say. 'Which is long enough.'

'It was my fault,' she says heavily. 'I put Callisto in there. I thought it would help.' She turns to my mother. 'I thought you would know peace there, that it would be easier. I didn't know you'd had a child. When I knew for sure who Clementine was, I spent days looking for you, but it was too late: Io had hidden you, and I couldn't find you anywhere.' Her voice shakes. She is braced for attack, drawn up tight, ready for her sisters to take her down.

But they don't. They just watch her unravel all by herself, lost and lonely in the house she made a prison.

'I'm sorry,' she says.

They're such small words, and her voice is so small as she says them. The house does not shake, the walls do not crack, but something shifts anyway, something quiet and warm that flowers into the air and picks up all their broken threads, and makes the air hum with the song of three sisters, joined together after a lifetime.

'Are you OK?' whispers Dylan, drawing me aside while they stare at each other, not speaking, not touching.

'I don't know,' I say. 'I don't know if we can make it right.'

'She can try,' he says. 'You can try. I would, if I had a chance. If my dad could come back . . .'

'You have memories; you knew he loved you!' I blurt.

'He was away half the year, and when he was around he was thinking of the sea. He wasn't perfect,' Dylan says. 'Nobody's perfect, Clem!'

'But you would try, if you had him back.'

'I would,' he says, holding on tight to Helios. 'And you will.'

'Will you, Clementine?' my mother asks. 'Can I make it up to you?' Her eyes fill. 'Tell me you always knew that I loved you . . . Tell me your pa told you, every day . . . Did he sing my song for you, even after I was gone?'

'Yes,' I say. 'But I didn't know it was a spell. I didn't

know about this place, about Ganymede or Io,' I say, my voice shaking. 'And I don't know why you hid me from them like that. Am I really so strange?'

'No,' she says. 'You are a wonder. You are a force of nature, magnified a million times. You are a whole world, all of yourself, far more than I could ever have imagined. I loved you so fiercely that I hardly knew what to do with myself when you slept, and I can say I'm sorry for the rest of my life, but it will never be enough. I don't know how to make it right.'

'Are you waiting for me to tell you?' I ask. 'Because I don't know!'

'You're right,' she says. 'It's up to me.' She nods firmly, and her song breaks out around her like a storm as she crosses the distance between us, making herself big around me as she holds me, her heart beating like a drum.

It's time. The sisters are doing a lot of flapping, and earnest talk, but they haven't worked out what Dylan and I have in mind. I doubt they've even considered it, even after everything that's happened. We don't debate it. We don't give them the chance to argue; it's just what needs to happen. What always needed to happen, ever since I first walked in here and found Dylan locked in a snowglobe.

Ever since we blew apart Io's globe, and felt the magic spiral out around us.

We start at the closest globes, joining our songs to break them. As each one smashes, there's a blast of power that makes the world just a tiny bit brighter, and the material within puffs out: clouds of tiny golden stars, coloured glitter, tiny gleaming blue fish – all bursting out like confetti. The magicians inside turn to us, their faces bright, and then they disappear.

'Where are they all going?' Dylan asks, after the third one.

'Back where they came from,' I say. 'That's what Fabia said. They'd all find their way . . .'

'Children!' comes a steely voice. 'What are you doing?'

'We're sending your prisoners home,' I say.

'Clementine, you can't just . . .' starts my mother.

'Chaos on the outside!' Io grins. 'How wonderful! Though, really, you can't imagine you'll break them all? Every single one? You'd change the whole world – who knows what would happen!'

'Don't tell me it can't be done,' Dylan whispers,

looking at her with flashing eyes. 'You have done a million things that should never have happened. Don't tell me this isn't possible. Why should any three people control all the magic of the world? How can you think it's right?'

'I . . . I don't,' Io stutters, lost for words. 'But the prisoners aren't all unhappy: they have their worlds, their magic; there are parties, celebrations . . .'

'It's all an illusion,' says Dylan. 'Nothing's real. Not the heat, or the food – none of the things they make in there. They all know that. I knew that.'

'I tried to help,' she says. 'I brought Helios to you. I even made a little house, but you wouldn't accept it. You didn't accept your magic, Dylan! I meant no harm. I went in there to help them all!'

Ganymede snorts. 'You went in there to get away from me.' She looks at Dylan. 'We locked those with magic away to keep the world safe. I saw you lose your temper; I saw how you denied your magic until it leaped out. It could have been a danger. We were supposed to—'

'No,' my mother interrupts, the flowers in her hair spreading like vines down her back, violet blooms opening with a powerful scent. 'Ganymede, you're wrong. We were supposed to *help* those who struggled with their magic. We weren't supposed to make a prison! Our parents were mistaken when they started to lock people away for showing a little talent with the wind, or the sea. And we made it worse!'

'So we're just supposed to let them all go back to their own realities?' Ganymede stares at her. '*All* of them?'

'Imagine it, Gan.' Io's golden cloak swirls as she turns. 'The whole world full of magic – full of the wonder of it!'

'The world is already full of wonder,' Ganymede says. 'This magic we're talking about has teeth, Io! Not every magician is good and kind, or very wise at all. We would be unleashing chaos.'

'But that's where it's supposed to be,' I say. 'Out there, with the rest of the chaos. Look at this house. Look at the cracks, the way the worlds turn and storm; it can't be contained here forever. All this magic isn't supposed to be locked away! You've taken it from the world and it's made you monsters!'

We stare at each other, she and I, and I see it suddenly: her fear of letting it all go. Of being left here alone, not even the snowglobes to give her a purpose.

You don't need it, I say. *You have family – isn't that better?*

'I don't know what you mean,' she whispers. 'I don't *have* you. People come and go. You will go home to your pa, at the end of this. Callisto will leave. And Io and I will fall out, we always do, and then she'll storm off, and I'll be here alone for another eternity!'

'Or . . . you could stop hiding the house,' Dylan says. 'Everybody knows there's something strange about this part of town, so let them see it. Go out once in a while, meet other people.'

'We can't just go out and about like *normal* people!' she gasps.

I laugh. I can't help it. She looks so horrified at the idea. She stares at me, and I try to swallow it, but it bursts, over and over, echoing through the corridor, making the globes swirl.

'I'm sorry,' I manage eventually. 'But yes you can. It might not be easy, but you can do it. I do it, every day!'

'But what would Papa say?' Ganymede asks, her eyes shining.

'It doesn't matter,' says my mother firmly, raising a hand and breaking a couple of snowglobes with a quick flash of her dark eyes.

Feathers and beads spill out into the corridor, and

Ganymede raises a hand to her mouth as the magicians within disappear.

'He was a good man, Gan, but he was mistaken about our purpose in all of this. He was supposed to be *teaching* those with magic, not imprisoning them – *that's* why this house was built. There were flaws, perhaps, but at least it was the right intention. Maybe we can return to it, some day, but for now it just needs to not be a prison any longer.' She picks up her skirts and starts to rush down the corridor ahead of us, snowglobes pinging as she goes, glitter and tiny foil shapes cascading out all around her. 'Come on!' she says, turning back with glittering eyes. 'Let's do it!'

30

The house is aglow with a mess of glitter and beads and bright golden stars. We have been through every room, broken every globe, sent every magician back to where they came from. And every time we do, the air gets lighter, the candles in the sconces brighter. By the time we reach the ground floor, we are exhausted and wired with adrenaline, and the house is full of sunlight.

Io and my mother dance between the study and the main front room; Dylan and Helios are in the kitchen, probably raiding cupboards for food more than bursting snowglobes; and Ganymede and I are in the main hall. The globes that line the shelves are in uproar, and the tiny figures press their hands and their foreheads to the glass, for they know what's coming; the whisper has been as loud as a tsunami. The tiny worlds that dangle from the ceiling on copper chains are swinging, tinkling as they brush against each other, and Ganymede is watching it all with a strange look on her face, angst and hope all tangled together.

'Ready?' I ask.

'Let's do it together, little snippet,' she says, taking a deep breath. 'All of them at once. If you will?'

She comes towards me and holds out her hands. They are less like claws now, as if letting go of so much has already softened her. Her question is uncertain, almost shy as she looks down at me. She is so tall, so strange, like the most beautiful, awkward bird you ever saw, all angles and feathers and sharp, staring eyes. I put my hands in hers, and she bites her lip. Her song is moon-soft and bright as silver. It brushes against me, waiting, tentative, and I realize I can't join her until I forgive her for everything that happened here. Until I do, it will not come.

I close my eyes, and let it go, piece by piece. The thing that held on to every difference, every mean word from Jago. The thing that settled over my skin like armour and pushed everyone away, that blamed this house for all my struggles, that blamed my mother for leaving me. It breaks, and the song comes tumbling out, joining with hers, spiralling out as her face brightens with hope. We stand together in the middle of the hallway and our power blooms out around us, the globes breaking with a chime that rings through the house.

Tiny shells and stones of every colour rain down around us – pine needles, silver flecks, foil fish and gleaming golden sand bursting out from every shelf. The vast front door bursts open as our song grows, joined by Io and my mother, and then Dylan, and a tide of it rushes out from our feet, spiralling down the steps, bursting out into the air, making the blue sky bluer, all the colours in the world brighter. Birds flit into the garden, their song joining ours, and all the tumult of the world bursts in. I can hear the traffic on the main road, the bell that rings as the door to the bakery opens. Ganymede's eyes widen as it rushes around us, as people stop and stare up at the house that was here before anything else, and hid among them for so long.

'What did we do?' she whispers.

'Chaos!' thrills Io, grabbing her arm and pulling her forward. 'Look at it, Ganymede! Come *out* of here and see!'

Her eyes sparkle as she pulls her sister on to the broad, shining steps, and my mother comes to stand by me, threading her arm through mine.

'*You* did this,' she says, her voice fierce. 'You changed everything, Clementine. Nobody else could have done this, not in all those hundreds of years. You are so like Gan, like all of us – only you could have shown her that it was nothing to be afraid of.' She catches at Dylan with her other arm and draws him near. 'You are both true magicians, full of heart, and that is a very lucky thing for me.'

I peer around her at Dylan. Despite all our adventures, he's looking better than he has since I first found him here. Perhaps it was all that power rushing around him; he couldn't help but breathe it in.

'You'll be even more magical now,' I say to him as my mother joins her sisters to look out at the world that now looks straight back in at them.

They are such a sight, in all their feathers and gold-spun robes, that the people on the street cannot help but stare. Helios sprawls before us in a patch of sunlight, keeping one eye on prowling Portia, and Dylan smiles, reaching into his pocket and pulling out the pale, round fruit that fell from my tree in his snowy world.

'So will you,' he whispers. 'It didn't disappear, Clem. It's a real fruit . . .'

I take it with a shaking hand. 'Look at that! We have magic, Dylan! Real, actual magic!'

'It's a good job,' he says. 'I need to convince Mum and Lionel they've always wanted a dog as big as a small horse to move in, and I might need a bit of help.'

THE END

Acknowledgements

My first thanks to go my brilliant, insightful editor Lucy Pearse, without whom this book might still be a shambles of mean unicorns and even meaner jelly babies. You saw the truth I was trying to get to before I did, and ever so patiently cleared away the hiding places I'd built for myself along the way, and I am grateful.

Thank you to everybody at Macmillan who works so hard to make all of this possible, especially to Jo Hardacre, Amber Ivatt, Kat McKenna and Jess Rigby. To Rachel Vale for designing a truly beautiful cover, and to Helen Crawford-White for such wonderful illustrations.

To my agent, Amber Caraveo, thank you for everything, but especially on this occasion for having absolute confidence in me when all I had was the wobblies.

A big thank you to all of the authors out there who have supported me and my books along the way, and to all of the bloggers and the teachers and the reviewers too. I am very lucky to have your support, and I hope you all know just how much I appreciate every tweet, every review, every kind word.

Thanks to my friends Caroline, Lu, Nikki, Jackie, Sam, Fiona, Hywel and Wibke and Julia and Sophie, for *everything*, and to Aviva, this time especially for your Granny's kitchen, which seems to be at the heart of all my fictional houses. (I'm afraid Ganymede made rather a mess of it on this occasion.)

Finally, thank you to my family: to my Mum Helen, and to Mike, to Judith and Charles, and to Lee, and Theia, Aubrey and Sasha. These acknowledgements are rather late getting to Lucy because I cannot find the right words to express what you mean to me, I'll just have to hope you know it anyway, through my actions if not my words.

About the Author

Amy Wilson has a background in journalism and lives in Bristol with her young family. She is a graduate of the Bath Spa MA in Creative Writing and is the author of the critically acclaimed novels *A Girl Called Owl* – longlisted for the Branford Boase Award and nominated for the CILIP Carnegie medal – and *A Far Away Magic*. *Snowglobe* is her third novel for Macmillan.

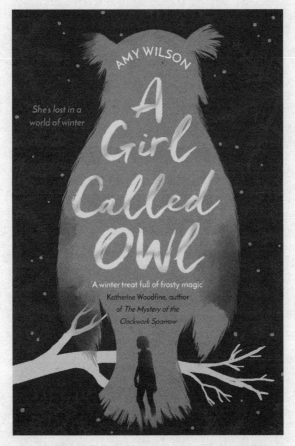

AMY WILSON

She's lost in a
world of winter

A
Girl
Called
Owl

A winter treat full of frosty magic
Katherine Woodfine, author
of *The Mystery of the
Clockwork Sparrow*

Owl has always wanted to know who her father is,
but when you've got a mum who won't tell you
anything and a best friend with problems of her own,
it's difficult to find time to investigate.

When Owl starts seeing strange frost patterns on her skin
and crying tears of ice, her world shifts. Could her strange
new powers be linked to the father she's never met?

'Original and compelling . . . an
unexpected tale of grief, magic and monsters'
Kiran Millwood Hargrave, author of
The Girl of Ink & Stars

AMY WILSON

A Far
Away
Magic

Both are lost –
magic will find them

'Original and compelling . . . an
unexpected tale of grief, magic and monsters'
Kiran Millwood Hargrave, author of
The Girl of Ink & Stars

When Angel moves to a new school after the death
of her parents, she isn't interested in making friends.
Neither is Bavar – he's too busy trying to hide.

But Bavar has a kind of magic about him, and Angel is
drawn to the shadows that lurk in the corners of his world.
Could it be that magic, and those shadows,
that killed her parents?